A deafening scream ripped through the apartment. There was then a moment of total silence, before everyone started to mutter and gobble and surge toward the bedroom door. Lady Margaret and Yale Dalton managed to arrive first. Marie d'Avalon stood with one hand outflung dramatically and the other to her mouth. She was staring at the open door to the bathroom.

Emma, Lady Ross, lay on her back on the white tile floor, with a purpled face and staring eyes. A thin strip of gray material—the belt to the robe she wore—was knotted around her neck. . . .

Also by Joyce Christmas
Published by Fawcett Books:

SUDDENLY IN HER SORBET

SIMPLY TO DIE FOR

A FÊTE WORSE THAN DEATH

Joyce Christmas

FAWCETT GOLD MEDAL • NEW YORK

A Fawcett Gold Medal Book
Published by Ballantine Books
Copyright © 1990 by Joyce Christmas

Library of Congress Catalog Card Number: 90-93044

ISBN 0-449-14665-0

Manufactured in the United States of America

First Edition: September 1990

For John Malone and Paul Baldwin

Chapter 1

"*Margaret!* *What* a treat! You must have thought I'd died."

Lady Margaret Priam's first thought before she turned to the voice was how tiresome it was that Emma Ross had managed to discover her in the middle of this particular crowd of black-tied, grandly gowned, culturally inclined New Yorkers.

Her second thought was that people like Emma, Lady Ross (as she styled herself on no sound basis that Margaret was aware of) do not live quietly, and they tend to depart this world with as much inconvenience as possible to everyone.

Then Margaret Priam, daughter of a peer of the realm, sister to the present earl, and undeniably a lady of birth and comportment, faced Emma Ross, with her (possibly assumed) title and fond (possibly fabricated) memories of her English country house childhood.

Since this was New York City, however, it didn't much matter, up to a point, what one called oneself or whether there had been armies of nannies in one's nursery. What mattered to everyone at this gala opening of a new exhibit at a large white art museum opposite Central Park was seeing and being seen by a great many people who were frequently other than they claimed to be.

Emma looked her usual winsome blue-eyed, fluffy blond

self, as she stood on tiptoe to touch cheeks with Margaret. Emma was too buxom and too short to be considered stylish, in the elongated and fleshless sense of the word, but she made up for it with a doll-like demeanor and flawless white skin and a total disregard for what others thought.

"You've been away then," Margaret said. She hadn't noticed Emma's absence—indeed, she hadn't encountered Emma in many months—but Emma didn't appear to mind.

"A perfectly lovely time abroad," Emma said. "Such a relief to get away on holiday." It was widely rumored that Emma Ross's holidays cost her remarkably little money. She had a gift for attracting free passage. Margaret noted that she had finally managed to overcome the occasional telltale Australian vowel that nobody else noticed. Americans weren't clever about the accents of the British Empire, nor about titles if it came to that. On the other hand, it was barely possible to picture Emma as the antipodean poppet bride of an aged titled Englishman who, in dying, had left her the dowager Lady Ross. Cagey Emma, however, had always been vague about her antecedents, although admittedly strong on the details of upper-class English life. All that served her well in her none-too-stately progress through the fringes of New York society.

"I don't think much of the pictures," Emma said. She waved upward to the sweeping swirl of ramps and white walls hung with the peculiar paintings of Fabrique Newton. "Isn't the artist very recently dead? Probably makes them all the more valuable. What do you think?" Emma peered at Margaret with an appealingly dim-witted expression that had fooled any number of people.

"I have taken no position on Fabrique Newton's artistic significance," Margaret said. "But I understand that if one had assisted in supporting his various addictions with cash in exchange for his pictures, one would be in a sound financial position today."

"I went all the way to the top to look at them, even before I had a glass of wine. I thought Yale ought to do the exhibit first. Wise, don't you think? You've seen it, you can honestly say so, and then you can mingle. Yale agrees. . . ."

"Yale?" Margaret's toleration of Emma's chatter had peaked. She looked around for her satisfyingly platonic friend, Prince Paul Castrocani, at whose invitation she had attended this gala opening. She had left him in pursuit of an attractive young woman whom he believed to be the principal heiress of a major American shopping mall magnate.

"Yale is one of my clients," Emma said, and shook herself with pleasure so that her very short and very ruffled frock shimmied. Emma Ross was probably about thirty, half a dozen years younger than Margaret, but Margaret's sleek blond elegance made Emma's mild excesses appear several notches below perfect taste.

"Client?" Margaret could not imagine that Emma had secured legal accreditation during her perfectly lovely trip abroad. Margaret recalled that when last they had met, Emma was about to apply to become a salesperson at Asprey's Trump Tower shop, to sell the odd thousand-dollar picnic basket or leather-bound portfolio to millionaires who wandered in off Fifth Avenue. Before that, she had toyed with the idea of real estate, having calculated the commission on two-million-dollar apartments. The prospect of qualifying examinations had soon halted her.

"Yale is a remarkable man," Emma said. "Self-made. A rough American diamond, but with tons of money and very clever about business and investing. Yet so innocent and open to new experiences. I met him in Geneva, quite lost. . . . "

"And he now is your client?"

"I thought surely you would have heard," Emma said, and pouted. "I'm doing public relations. I started out helping a friend or two who wanted to make their names better known, and it was so terribly promising that I've taken on something bigger. Out-of-town businessmen who are opening offices in New York and need to know the right sort of people. The art of self-promotion is so American, but *so* important, don't you agree?"

Margaret was well aware that Emma was living proof of the value of self-promotion. But she was harmless enough, and had been quite kind to Margaret a few years earlier, when Margaret had only just arrived in New York from England and had not yet found a circle of congenial friends, nor had yet been taken up by the social set enamored of accents and titles.

"I agree," Margaret said. "It's the only way to get ahead. Look at poor Fabrique Newton. He would probably be nowhere had he not promoted his art into the headlines via his sordid death."

"Aren't you doing some sort of arty thing?" Emma asked. Her attention was beginning to wander. Her large limpid eyes darted rapidly around the room, picking out the well-known faces, tabulating them, assessing chances for an invitation or two for dinner or drinks.

"I continue to work with Bedros Kasparian at his shop," Margaret said, "although I don't know if flogging bits of Oriental antiquity is truly arty. Honest work, at least, since Kasparian sells the real thing."

"What fun!" Emma chirped insincerely. "Much more satisfying than my work. Stuffy business meetings and soothing the tempers of persons who feel they know more about all this than I. Ah, here's Yale. Yale . . ." Emma's voice rose. "Come meet Lady Margaret Priam, a very dear old friend from home."

Margaret took the hand of the man Emma introduced as Yale Dalton. He was tall and lean, with a leathery tan that spoke of years rather than a mere holiday in the sun. Margaret guessed he was in his forties. For a rough diamond, his evening clothes were quite flawless. Perhaps Emma had helped, but in any event, Margaret hoped that he kept his credit cards locked up when Emma was about.

"Yale is from . . ." Emma paused and batted her lashes at the man. "I am simply terrible with American cities."

"I'm from out West," Yale Dalton said. "Not much for cities." He had a hint of a western drawl that Margaret recognized from her Texas acquaintances.

"Emmy here has sorta taken me in hand, showing me the ropes in New York City," Yale said. "I sure am pleased to meet ya."

Margaret hoped his guileless-country-boy-in-the-wicked-city act was not for her benefit. He was Emma's "client."

"She's a real go-getter, Emma is," Yale Dalton said. "Knows all the best folk."

"Indeed she does," Margaret said. "Lovely to see you, Emma. Mr. . . . um, Dalton. My escort seems to be signaling me."

Margaret managed to edge away graciously from Emma and party, and headed through the crowd toward Paul Castrocani. Scarcely three steps into the crowd, she felt Emma's soft little hand grasp her arm.

Emma whispered, "Are you here with anybody serious? I mean to say, I understood you were seeing some sort of . . ." Emma hesitated. "Some sort of person . . ." she concluded weakly.

"I see several people," Margaret said serenely, "and my escort tonight is strictly a friend." If Margaret preferred to spend her quality time with a quirky but engaging police detective who refused to go about in society, that was surely not Emma's business.

Emma continued to whisper. "Would you be free then to come for drinks on Friday? A few friends, and some business people. It would be a great favor." Emma sounded pleading, and again Margaret remembered that she had been kind during those first lonely months in New York. It was only later that she had become tiresome.

"I could arrange it," Margaret said cautiously.

"I'll call you," Emma said, and seemed delighted. She tippy-toed back to Yale and grasped his arm. They forged a way into the crowd, with Emma scattering introductions and greetings about like so many rose petals to people who were not sure who she was. Her client indeed. Margaret wasn't quite buying that.

"I would be willing to depart," Paul Castrocani said, "unless you would care to view the pictures." He shook his fine Roman head. Prince Paul Castrocani cut an elegant figure, though barely past his mid-twenties. "I myself do not understand them."

"Let's stop and chat with Dianne Stark a moment," Margaret said. "Then we leave, and I take you to dine." Although Paul's Texas mother was indecently rich, she kept the product of her defunct marriage to an Italian prince on a tight allowance.

Dianne Stark had married an older man high in New York financial circles and had become a delightful hostess, something she credited to her years as a flight attendant. She immediately invited Margaret and Paul to an informal buffet at the Starks' Park Avenue apartment after the opening.

"Charlie did something marvelous with money a couple of days ago, and we're celebrating. Maybe you read about it in *The Wall Street Journal*?"

"I must have missed it," Margaret said. "But don't you look pure glamour tonight." There was a touch of envy in her voice; bias-cut satin suited Dianne, but alas not Margaret or many others.

"This old thing . . . It *is* nice though, isn't it?" Dianne said. "Kendall Smith designed it for me before he got so grand, and his dresses turned rather bizarre. An awful lot of beading and feathers and embroidery. I wonder how any woman can carry around the weight of all those rhinestones. I see you were talking to Emma Ross, Lady Whatsit." She laughed. "Needless to say, she and that man she has in tow are not invited tonight. She's dying to have him meet Charlie, but the least I can do for my husband is spare him Emma Ross."

"You're turning into a terrible gossip," Margaret said mildly. "Emma is merely trying to make her way in a cruel city."

"True enough. But did I ever tell you I once saw her look at the hallmark on a silver teaspoon—it was years ago at poor Basil Jones's place—and put it in her bag as calmly as can be? You know about Emma as well as I do; never pay if you can get it for free, borrow if it will not be given, and take what isn't a gift or a loan if you fancy it." Dianne shrugged. "I won't tolerate it, but you're far better at *noblesse oblige* than I. Did you never find some little thing oddly missing upon her departure from your place?"

"Certainly not," Margaret said, but one or two small objects had gone missing around the time when Emma used to drop in for a chat. Margaret had chosen not to notice.

"You don't lie well, Margaret." Dianne turned to Paul. "Paul dear, I believe the cook planned *tartufo* for one of the desserts this evening. That's a nice reminder of your homeland. And you must tell me what beautiful young heiress you are pursuing this week."

"I believe my mother wishes me to marry the daughter of someone who owns cows," Paul said.

"In Texas, that would be cattle, I think," Dianne said. "And who is the young lady?" Dianne, it should be said, had long imagined that Prince Paul and her younger sister from Rhode Island would make a handsome couple.

"She has no one specific in mind," Paul said. "She is merely thinking about consolidating her financial position. A dynastic union, in the way marriages used to be arranged among my princely Roman ancestors."

Margaret caught sight of a flurry at the entrance—Emma had flung a wrap about her shoulders, had dropped her little handbag, had summoned waiters and Yale Dalton and innocent bystanders to gather up her scattered belongings.

"Ah," Margaret said. "Emma departs with her rough diamond. It doesn't appear that she is thinking of crashing your gathering this evening."

"Have you ever wondered what Emma does think of, when she's alone?" Dianne asked. "Does she try to remember how she came by that phony title and that *terribly* British accent and those names she likes to drop—the archduke, the comtesse, the bishop, the governor. . . ."

"She's harmless," Margaret said. "And, really, I don't believe she thinks much at all."

Chapter 2

Margaret and Dianne were wrong. Emma Ross did think, especially when she was alone.

On the Wednesday before her little gathering, she thought about explaining to the food shop where she planned to order pretty trays of hors d'oeuvres for Friday night that she was terribly sorry, she'd misplaced her credit card, but they knew her . . . Lady Ross, and please deliver by five at the very latest. She'd pay by check—which would certainly be covered by Yale Dalton's promised retainer for her services before there was any unpleasantness at the bank where there were now no funds, and no hope of an overdraft.

She thought with pleasure about the really good Kendall Smith at-home gown she managed to borrow from an acquaintance to whom it had not occurred that Emma wouldn't hesitate to take up the hem (just a few inches) to suit her height. Kenny himself had more than once told her she was wrong for his important gowns, and absolutely refused to loan her a thing, in spite of the good she'd done him.

Now and then, Emma even thought about the superintendent of her barely adequate (and curiously empty) apartment in a building on quite a nice block on the upper East Side. She hoped he would not be moved to present her with an eviction notice at the height of her party, to punish her for ignoring his hints that he'd like to be invited in. In any case, she was only a month behind in the rent.

Emma often thought a good deal about the tiresome concerns of the present—even though it was only money, and someone would provide. She sometimes thought happily about the future, but not at all about the past.

On that Wednesday morning, Emma sat at a narrow dropleaf table in her living room and chewed a pencil as she pondered her list of guests. Many names were crossed off, a few inserted. There were quite a few question marks. Not everyone was eager to do Emma a tiny favor.

She looked up expectantly at the sound of the clicking lock on the apartment door.

"Nicky?"

As the door opened slowly, a tall, stooped, and regal old man entered the apartment. He had longish white hair yellowed about the edges, and he wore a flowing black cloak. Now being the start of autumn, it was perhaps the only time of the year when such garb did not look entirely peculiar in the daytime.

"Hard at your work, are you?" The old man hid his key away in a pocket somewhere in the folds of his cloak and tottered cautiously across the polished floor to a somewhat shabby armchair near Emma.

"It's shaping up well," Emma said. She gazed about the sparsely furnished room. "With enough people and plenty of candlelight, it will be quite jolly."

"You'll surely have flowers. You must have flowers."

"Of course I will, old darling." But she had forgotten the flowers, and was quickly calculating that she probably had sufficient cash to buy a couple of prepackaged bouquets from the Korean vegetable-flower-salad-bar shop at the corner. The mainstream florist up the block was far too pricey. "Lady Margaret Priam has absolutely promised to come. Firm promise. I just rang her, and I made it clear I wanted her alone, no beau to distract her."

"Margaret Priam? The Priams have a large estate in England, I recall. I met her father years ago. The earl of something. He was rude, and claimed that he could never understand what foreigners were saying.'' Archduke Niklas had an odd accent that came and went, depending on the subject. On the subject of English peers, he sounded like the master of a large drafty castle in the middle of a long-decayed duchy in an outré corner of central Europe. ''I hope she is more gracious.''

''Well . . .'' Emma put down her pencil and stood up. ''She's all right. High and mighty airs, and a bit old for my purposes. She must be at least thirty-five, but still attractive. And American men like blondes, even older ones.''

''It doesn't become you to be unkind, especially in view of your present associates, who are nothing to boast of,'' Archduke Niklas said crossly. ''And it does not become you, even at home alone, to be wearing a robe in that condition. You do not know who might be calling.''

Emma looked down at her tatty gray bathrobe and the scuffed mules with fur trim that had seen better days. ''The Archduke Niklas's cultural counselor has a bare closet just now,'' she said. ''And too much on her mind to think about dressing. Besides, no one is likely to visit without phoning. You forget how useful the telephone is, since you refuse to have one.''

Archduke Niklas sighed and sat back in his chair. ''An unnecessary expense.'' His back was straight and he held his head high. The casual observer might readily believe that he was the last of an ancient ruling line, living in diminished circumstances.

''You're right, old dear,'' she said finally, seeing that he was displeased. ''Keep up the standards, and all that.'' Then she added offhandedly, but with an eye on the old man, ''I've invited Norman Hope and his dreadful wife.''

He looked at her for a moment, then shook his head. ''Not wise, not wise at all. Even if the liaison has ended, and you claimed the wife never knew . . .''

''She couldn't know. Norman swore she didn't, and it was all rather a mistake. I was so terribly broke, and Norman wanted to help me. How could I refuse?'' There was no answer to that, but Emma contrived to look forlorn and innocent. "Besides, Norman is willing to be useful to Yale for my sake."

"His own sake seems more likely," the archduke muttered.

"In any case, they've accepted. Belinda Hope is always desperate for invitations to anything that has a few decent names. With Lady Margaret coming, and the Comtesse d'Avalon . . ."

The archduke grimaced. "Comtesse, indeed. A wayward American with a taste for the high life. So different from her mother. I was very fond of her mother years ago in Paris. I've told you that, haven't I?"

"You've told me," Emma said. "Many times. You know that Marie was married for some months to the comte. You even awarded him an order for his services."

"Only the Golden Goblet and Swords, third class," Nicky said. "He did me a financial favor. And I remind you that there is doubt that he came by his title honestly, and then the marriage was annulled, so why she continues to call herself countess . . ."

"I don't have time to argue, Nicky. Marie is *quite* a dear friend, and I shall always make allowances for her. She is being most helpful to us lately, as you well know. Now, I have a few more things to pack up for you to take away. Just a small box of papers and bibelots I can't bear to part with. They'll be in a Saks shopping bag in the bedroom."

"Is there lunch?" The archduke sounded hopeful.

"A little something for you, at least. I'm lunching with Yale at his hotel at one." She shook her curls and looked pleased. "We're going to discuss all the plans, and everything will be settled. One or two papers are to be signed by you. I told you about that."

"Yes, well . . . I should have to read them carefully before I sign. I do not entirely trust Mr. Dalton."

Emma very nearly frowned. "Don't worry so. He's absolutely all right, and I am managing everything very nicely, thank you. He likes me very much, you know."

"Emma, do not pin romantic hopes on this man. I do not

believe we know enough about him. He is presentable enough. . . ."

"Oh, Nicky! I am not speaking of romance! I'm talking about business. Yours and mine. And the others. Everyone is going to come out of this undertaking very well off."

"Can he be as prosperous as he claims? When a man wants something as useless as a bit of bone-dry desert, I doubt his sanity and possibly his honesty." The archduke could well have been speaking from decade upon decade of experience.

"Yale has shown me ever so many papers and prospectuses and balance sheets. Buy-outs and buy-ins. And he needs land to . . . to . . . I forget precisely, but it has something to do with attracting investors and such. It's quite simple."

"I do not understand." Archduke Niklas was sadly regal. "I am too old to understand."

"Nonsense. You're not at all old," Emma said, a gracious liar when necessary. She pulled her robe around her and shivered. "The building is simply awful about heat. I'll fetch you a nice cup of tea. You look tired. Are you feeling well?"

"Don't fuss so, Emma. I am *old*, I tell you, and that is sufficient to tire any man."

She patted his wrinkled old hand. "Soon we'll go off to live in some lovely place where it's always warm," she said. "Monte Carlo, perhaps. You'd like that. You can go to the casino and fascinate the ladies, the way you used to." She shivered. "I can't imagine why anyone chooses to live in New York forever."

"They do so because it is the city of opportunity, my dear, for those that play the game well. I reveled in the game when I came here years ago, but I feel of late that my game is ending. At least I've had the pleasure of seeing you make your mark. If there is no obstacle as yet unseen."

Emma looked at him sharply, but he had leaned back in his chair and closed his eyes. So she said nothing and went to the tiny kitchen to put the tea water on to boil.

When she had settled Archduke Niklas with tea and a thin sandwich, Emma donned a neat, businesslike suit that might almost be mistaken for the creation of one of the big names in fashion. By now, Nicky was dozing, the sandwich half-eaten, the tea growing cold. She patted his hand affectionately, but he barely stirred.

"Back by six," she wrote with a flourish on the back of an envelope that had contained her monthly statement from Bloomingdale's with a sharp reminder that no payment had been received for the previous month. She left the note beside the tea mug.

By Friday evening, she thought, the pieces would be in place. A few more details to arrange, some people to see, some loose ends to tie up. Emma had almost completed orchestrating a financial triumph for herself and the dear old archduke.

She paused at the little gilt mirror beside the door and liked what she saw: pretty, clever Emma, Lady Ross, who was able to make everyone happy. The mirror also showed her the distant reflection of the frail Niklas as he might have napped in archducal splendor in ancient halls. The dear man was too suspicious. She could handle Yale Dalton and the rest. The dazzling prospect of wealth was not to be dimmed by the knowledge that perhaps she was sometimes less than honest about the business she was involved in.

Then Emma set out to arrange her financial destiny, never doubting that it would all be as she had planned.

Chapter 3

*O*n *Friday* evening, at six-thirty, Margaret stepped from the elevator on Emma's floor and saw an open door at the end of the corridor to her left. As she approached, the rumble of conversation confirmed that a gathering was in progress, and yes, the door carried the number the somewhat distracted doorman had told her to look for if she were a guest at "the Lady Ross's."

The corners of the room were dim, but tall candles massed on a table pushed against a wall lighted an array of prettily garnished platters and ranks of bottles and glasses. A dozen men and women were standing about in conversational clusters juggling their wine and bits of food. Margaret stood in the doorway and searched for Emma. Then Yale Dalton raised a hand in greeting and left the broad, beefy man he was talking to.

"It's Lady . . . Margaret—I got it right I think?"

"Mr. Dalton," Margaret said. "How pleasant to see you again."

"Jes' let me take your coat, and I'll have you meet some good old friends of mine."

"Emma?" Margaret said. "Isn't she here?"

"She had to run out. Left a note saying she'd be right back. That's what one of the folks was saying when I got here. She should be walkin' in any minute now." He took her coat and

14

hung it in a closet with sliding doors at one end of the room. "I'd be pleased to have you meet my associate. Wayne boy! Here's as pretty a lady as you'll ever meet."

The big man who looked to be somewhere in his fifties ducked his head shyly and put out his hand. "Wayne D. Wayne, ma'am. It's a pleasure."

"Margaret Priam," Margaret said. Another good old Western boy, she thought, with sinking heart. He was wearing one of those string ties held together by a silver eagle with a malignant turquoise eye.

"Ah'm in the all bidnis," Wayne D. Wayne said, and watched her expectantly.

"Lovely," she said, and waited, but enlightenment did not come. "The all bidnis," she murmured.

"Society could not get on without all," he said. "Cars would stop, plastics would stop, no heat for you poor folk who got to live in the snow. . . ."

"Oil!" Margaret said. "Of course. The oil business!" She felt as though she had solved a major mystery.

"This here's Tina Corrado." He pushed forward a young woman who put up her dark hair in a sensible bun and wore a serious navy dress with a string of pearls. She gazed at Margaret, then held out a soft, limp hand. "Tina is Yale's right-hand woman. Great little administrator," Wayne D. Wayne said heartily. "Ain't that right, Yale?"

"Couldn't get along without her," Yale said. "Would y'all excuse us for one second? I see some pals of mine are arrivin'." He herded Wayne D. Wayne toward two new arrivals. Margaret winced: Belinda and Norman Hope were not her favorite people, but there would be no avoiding them at this small gathering.

Tina watched Margaret silently. Margaret in turn tried desperately to think of something to say, or at least how she could gracefully remove herself to the drinks table. There were one or two familiar faces in the room. Marie d'Avalon was overpowering a bewildered young man, and there was that very old man one saw about who claimed to be the last gasp of some minor European royalty that had lost its country sometime in the course of the twentieth century. She understood he made his way by conferring titles on worthy people who showed their gratitude by conferring a worthy cash donation on him.

"Is this your first visit to New York, Miss Corrado?" Margaret finally said, and was answered with only a nod.

Margaret tried again. "And how do you like the city?"

Tina said, "I'm not accustomed to this kind of life. Lady Ross says I must get over my shyness to . . . to succeed here."

Margaret took a closer look at her. She seemed more self-contained than shy, and she might be rather more attractive than she appeared. A little makeup, clothes with a bit more style, and she'd be quite pretty. Yale returned to Margaret's side with the Hopes in tow. "This here is Mister Norman Hope and the missus," he said.

"Margaret, what a surprise to see *you* here." Belinda Hope looked Margaret up and down critically. She clung to her husband's arm and managed to turn their backs on Yale and his colleagues. Yale took the hint and moved Tina and Wayne away to chat up the other guests.

Margaret knew the Hopes slightly, but definitely knew that gossip had it that Belinda would stop at nothing to promote Norman's Wall Street career and their mutual social careers.

"We only accepted Emma's invitation because she promised some people Norman ought to meet," Belinda said in a low voice. "I hope she didn't mean that hick." She tossed her bountiful hair in Yale Dalton's direction. "Although you never know who has assets nowadays." Belinda, Margaret noticed, was not admitting publicly that Dalton already considered the Hopes "good pals."

"I am surprised that Emma is absent at her own party," Margaret said.

· Norman said suddenly, "She's scatterbrained. I found that out when I tried to help put her financial affairs in order."

"Financial affairs," Belinda repeated. "Financial *affairs*."

"Belinda . . ." Norman said. Margaret heard the pleading voice of a man who had listened to that tone many, many times.

Belinda smiled brightly. "She'll turn up. She always does. I did notice that the Comtesse d'Avalon is here. I understand she and Emma are very close. She's truly glamorous, don't you think?"

Margaret thought Marie usually dressed like a trollop, but glamour is in the eye of the beholder. In an effort to detach herself from the Hopes, Margaret said, "Perhaps I'll ask if she knows where Emma has got to."

"The comtesse is talking to the Archduke Niklas," Norman said grandly. "What a charming old gentleman, what a life he has led. He and Emma have become very close, you know." A look from Belinda halted further comment on the archduke or Emma.

"He is . . . a phenomenon," Margaret said. She saw Marie d'Avalon slipping through a doorway that led to the bedroom. True to form, she displayed excessive bosom and a doubtful fashion sense. She had likely gone to powder her nose in the bathroom of the mistress of the house, rather than in the loo off the kitchen. Margaret had a good recollection of Emma's apartment from the days when they used to have tea and pretend to reminisce about the England of Margaret's childhood, if not Emma's.

"I'll just mingle a bit, and we'll all have a nice chat later." Margaret edged away from the Hopes, and was relieved to catch sight of Kendall Smith, the dress designer, peering cautiously into the apartment from the hall. Here was someone she could speak to without pretense. Kenny was wildly self-centered and ambitious, but civilized and amusing. She moved in his direction.

Kendall Smith had raised the appearance of blond elfin bespectacled bemusement to a high art, but some of his couture dresses were clever, albeit remarkably expensive. He himself invariably wore a neat blue blazer and gray trousers and resembled an escapee from a fairly good boys' school.

"Margaret darling," he said, "what a relief to see a friendly face." He came into the room and surveyed it. "It looks a fairly dullish affair." Then he took her arm and guided her to a corner. "It's been ages since we're run into each other. You must have heard that I've been madly busy."

Margaret's blank look prompted him to continue. "My book for one thing."

"Ah, yes. I'd heard," Margaret said. "Fashion, is it?"

"Just about the best on the subject. *Feathers and Fashion Through History*. It's finished, printed, bound. I'm thrilled. Such good publicity for me. You're coming to my publication party, aren't you? Emma got Belinda Hope to organize it. That's one thing Emma managed to do right. God! There she is!"

Margaret turned to greet Emma at last, but Kendall's sharp blue eyes behind his round glasses had sighted only Belinda.

"I do hate having to play best friends with Belinda," he said under his breath, "but it's all in a good cause. Darling!" he chirped at Belinda across the room. She headed their way. "She's *not* wearing a Kendall," he said. "She promised."

Margaret said, "Emma persuaded Belinda? But Norman was . . ."

"One must remain civilized, dear heart, no matter with whom one's spouse carries on. Emma was handling matters for me. . . ."

Before Margaret could determine what those matters might be, a deafening scream ripped through the apartment. There was then a moment of total silence, before everyone started to mutter and gobble and surge toward the bedroom door. Margaret and Yale Dalton managed to arrive first. Marie d'Avalon stood with one hand outflung dramatically and the other to her mouth. She was staring at the open door to the bathroom.

"Keep everyone out," Margaret said over her shoulder to Yale, and brushed past Marie, who was uttering breathy little shrieks.

Emma, Lady Ross, lay on her back on the white tile floor, with a purpled face and staring eyes. A thin strip of gray material—the belt to the robe she wore—was knotted around her neck.

"Oh my God," Yale said behind Margaret. Then, loudly and briskly, "Ya'll just go back outside now. Marie hon, you just sit down. Hey there, Tina. Come look after the countess. She looks like she's goin' to faint."

Margaret backed away from the awful sight in the bathroom.

Yale was still giving instructions. "You there, fella. I wouldn't think of leaving just yet." Margaret heard Belinda Hope's shrill protest, and Yale's firm response: "Now, now, settle down. I'll be seein' to you in a minute."

Margaret squeezed her eyes shut, and then looked again at the late and perhaps unlamented Emma. Her robe was shabby and utilitarian and was open to show that Emma was wearing beautiful silk peach underwear with white lace. A deep rose chiffon gown with flowing sleeves and intricate silver embroidery at the neckline was hung carefully on a hanger hooked over the top of the bathroom door. Even in the shock of the moment, Margaret wondered how Emma could afford it: it looked like a Kendall Smith. On Emma's feet were delicate silver sandals with very high heels. It appeared that she had carefully made up her face, although under the circumstances it was not easy to tell. Margaret turned around. Marie had swooned artfully and had been laid out on the bed by an expressionless Tina.

"Tina, please call the police at once, if Mr. Dalton hasn't done so, and don't use the phone in this room," Margaret said.

"What has happened?" A quavery old voice, a frightened voice, spoke up behind Margaret. She turned quickly and managed to shield the view of Emma from Archduke Niklas.

"An accident, sir," Margaret said. She wasn't sure how one addressed a probably *faux* aristocrat with an excessively grand title. "Please go back to the drawing room."

"Is dear Emma all right?" He sounded so lost and pathetic that Margaret felt compelled to push him gently away.

"I'm not sure," she lied. Yale Dalton returned. "Please take the archduke away," she said. "Have the police . . . ?"

"Yes, ma'am," he said. "Terrible thing . . ." He took Archduke Niklas's arm firmly and steered him away.

"A terrible thing indeed," Margaret muttered to herself. "And what is De Vere going to say?" Margaret's policeman friend had forbidden her ever again to become involved in murder. But surely this was *not* her fault.

Margaret looked more closely at the dress hanging in the bathroom, then at a tiny label sewn into the back of the neckline. Definitely a Kendall Smith, but horror! Emma seemed to have taken up the hem rather crudely with large, untaut stitches. So much for Emma's claims of an upper-class English upbringing. One's nanny would have so drilled in the niceties of hemming that even in haste, one could not do such a sloppy job. There was a bluish smudge on the neckline as well. Unthinkable.

She made certain that Marie d'Avalon continued in her apparently genuine swoon, then looked quickly around the bedroom. Although she did not touch anything, she noticed a lot, and saw very little. The dressing table held only a comb and a single, nearly empty perfume bottle. There was a small zippered makeup case on the chair. It was open, and she noted an eyeliner, mascara, eye shadow in several shades, a pinkish lipstick.

The closet door was ajar. No doubt Marie had taken the opportunity to inspect the premises before retiring to the bathroom and the remains of Emma. Margaret edged the door open with her toe. There were many bare hangers, and only a few bits of clothing. One pair of low-heeled shoes on the floor. She returned the door to its original position. This was a room from which belongings had been removed. There were no papers in evidence, no books. There was no handbag. No little jewelry box on the bureau. She threw caution aside and opened a drawer, using the edge of her dress to cover the knob as she pulled. The drawer contained only a jumble of silky lingerie, some pale pastel, others a rich medley of bright greens and blues. The second drawer was empty.

If a robber, say, had surprised Emma while she was dressing, he had done a very neat job of removing everything. Impossibly neat.

The tension in the living room was palpable. They all looked intently at Margaret when she appeared. No one wanted to be there; no one wanted to admit that Emma Ross was anything more than a casually met person who had forced an invitation upon each of them. No one spoke to anyone else, except Belinda Hope, who was whispering furiously to Norman.

Kendall flew to Margaret. "What has the silly bitch done now? Done away with herself? I knew that things were often rather touch-and-go for her financially, but she was full of her new scheme—investments and that Dalton man. But she got depressed so easily. Was it an overdose?"

"Not precisely," said Margaret, who couldn't recall ever seeing Emma depressed by anything.

Uniformed police arrived: one young man who seemed confused by the scene before him, and a petite, tough young woman, who looked as though she had already seen it all. With a commanding flick of her hand, the woman officer sent Kendall Smith and the rest of Emma's guests to the far side of the room. Margaret alone stood her ground.

"Officer," Margaret said to the woman. She faced Margaret, her hand resting on the revolver on her hip.

"Yeah?" No nonsense here. "Suppose you get over there."

"Certainly," Margaret said. "It's just that—well, I believe I should speak to you first."

"They said it was a murder. Are you going to confess? If so, I'll read you your rights. . . . You English?"

"Yes," Margaret said, and felt guilty. The name on the officer's badge was Kelly, and one knew how the Irish felt about the English. "I mean, yes, I'm English, but I am not going to confess."

"Right. Sanchez, find the body, will you? And *please* don't touch anything this time."

"It's through there, in the bathroom," Margaret said helpfully.

Officer Kelly looked Margaret over. "Is anybody going to start shooting? Anything like that?"

"I think not," Margaret said. "It appears that the death occurred before anyone arrived. The guests believed that the hostess had gone out on an errand, whereas she was lying dead in there. Strangled. Or so it seems."

"You saw the victim? Did anyone call a doctor? Was she robbed? Raped?"

Margaret winced. "I don't know. She is quite definitely dead. Purple," she added reluctantly. "Rather awful."

Officer Kelly looked at her sadly, as though Margaret had no idea what "awful" actually was. Officer Sanchez beckoned. "I'll take a look. Sanchez, keep an eye on these . . ." She didn't quite say suspects. She went into the bedroom, leaving her partner to glare at the huddled guests. Margaret hoped the homicide detectives and the technical people arrived soon. She had seen a couple of unfortunate demises in the past, and preferred to speak to the man in charge.

"Hey, you . . ." Kelly stood at the bedroom door. "This dame isn't dead, she's just unconscious."

"The Comtesse d'Avalon discovered the body," Margaret said, "and was overcome. Look in the bathroom."

Officer Kelly came back, her uniform cap tucked under her arm while she wrote in a small leather-bound notebook. "She's dead, all right. Probably for a while." Kelly eyed Margaret with some suspicion. "How do you know so much about this?"

"I know nothing," Margaret said. "Do you know Detective De Vere?"

"I know of him," Kelly said. "Is he your friend in high places who'll get you out of this mess?"

"He's a friend," Margaret admitted.

"Here's Detective Russo," Kelly said. "He'll have to do instead of your De Vere."

A homicide detective Margaret had met previously in connection with another unexpected death came into the apartment. His eyes met hers in vague recognition, then he summoned the two uniformed officers for a whispered conference. A couple of men who carried equipment bags edged into the apartment, and Margaret caught a glimpse of a bulging, sour-faced man in a plaid shirt peering into the room from the doorway.

Detective Russo said, "Okay, everybody settle down. Let's find out what's happened. Don't I know you?" he said to Margaret.

"You might remember . . ." she began. She started again, "I go on record as stating that I looked at Lady Ross's body, saw that she was dead, told everyone not to touch anything, and had the police called.''

"A perfect little citizen," Russo said. He and Officer Kelly went to view the remains, followed by the evidence men. The man in the plaid shirt continued to survey the room from the doorway. Margaret imagined that he was the building super, drawn in by the sensation and at the same time annoyed at the fact of murder in his building.

Then, to her relief, De Vere appeared in the hallway behind the super, pushed past him, and came directly to her. He was not pleased, but Margaret was glad to see him.

"It's not my fault," Margaret said quickly. "I merely came for drinks. She was dead. No one knew she was there in the bathroom all the time. It must have happened long before people started arriving."

"What am I going to do with you?" De Vere said. He was expressionless, but Margaret knew him well enough to know that he was worried.

Margaret said the first thing that came into her head: "Marry me and take me away from all this?"

"I might have to," De Vere said. "I understand Russo is here and has taken charge. They won't like it. . . ." He indicated the guests who were being patrolled by Sanchez. They were beginning to mutter angrily. There were few chairs, and the drinks table was on the other side of the room. "No, they won't like it at all, but I'm going to remove you at once."

"But I don't want to miss . . ."

"Margaret," De Vere said sternly. "Stop it at once." Their eyes met. He was so cool, so casual, so appealing. He wore his customary immaculate jeans, shined loafers, and tonight, a gray tweed sport jacket over a crisp blue dress shirt, unbuttoned at the collar.

Russo and Kelly emerged from the murder room. He stopped when he saw Margaret with De Vere. "I shoulda remembered you. That woman who was murdered a while back. You were there."

"Listen here, officer," Belinda Hope said loudly from her side of the room. "I can't be expected to . . ."

Russo silenced her with a look.

Yale Dalton separated himself from the guests and approached Russo. "I beg pardon, sir, but my friends here hope to get this cleared up real fast. Yale Dalton at your service . . ."

"Mr. Dalton. Out-of-towner?" Russo, who was short, looked up at Dalton, who was tall.

"Sure am," Yale said. "Lady Ross was a good old gal, and I'm real sorry she's dead, but nobody here knew a thing about it. Isn't that right, Lady Margaret?"

"Well, I . . ."

Russo said, "I'm afraid I have to follow procedures, Mr. Dalton."

"Russo, I'm taking Lady Margaret away for questioning," De Vere said. Russo nodded with a straight face. The rumble of displeasure from the group of irritated members of midlevel New York society grew louder. Special treatment was much craved for themselves and bitterly resented for others.

De Vere took Margaret's arm. "Let them eat cake," he said to her. "If the murderer wasn't someone who came at the deceased's invitation, then it will be a drug-crazed delivery boy or . . ." He eyed the building super, who still hovered at the doorway and shrank back at De Vere's look. "Or the amorous and rejected super. Come along, Margaret, before you are arrested for being well dressed."

"Wait," Margaret said. "That old man over there. He calls himself Archduke Niklas. He's a fraud, but look at him. He's fading fast. Could you have him sent home with a guard? He doesn't look like the murderer of the piece. I don't think he'd have the strength to strangle a healthy young woman like Emma."

De Vere stopped. "Strangled? Is that what happened?"

"Perhaps you should view the body. And then do something about the archduke."

"All right," De Vere said. A few moments later, he was back at Margaret's side. "Your archduke is not under serious suspicion, although he claims to be the first person to arrive. He has a key, it seems. Very cozy. He says there was a note saying she'd be back at six sharp. He confesses to a nip of brandy and a bite of the Camembert. Then several people arrived, and they all waited for Lady Ross.

"Will they lock him up?" Margaret asked. The archduke seemed bewildered by the questions Russo was asking him.

"Not immediately," De Vere said. "He says he has a cape in the closet. Do you understand what he means?"

"I think so," she said. "Will we take him home?"

"It's way over on the West Side on Riverside Drive, as I understand it," De Vere said. "He seems confused."

Archduke Niklas, released by Russo, tottered toward them.

"Come along, sir," De Vere said. "Lady Margaret will find your cape." Man-of-the-people Sam De Vere had settled on "sir" as easily as Margaret had. Well, one never knew who a person might turn out to be when the geneologies came home to roost. Margaret found the cape hanging next to hers, along with a few other coats.

"A terrible thing has happened, Harry," the archduke said in a quavery voice to the super who was still standing in the doorway. "I'm not certain what. . . ."

Margaret and De Vere hustled the archduke toward the elevators.

"I don't understand all this," Archduke Niklas said. "Is Emma ill? No one would tell me."

"I cannot lie, sir," Margaret said. "She is very ill."

"Such a beautiful girl," he said. "So kind. I knew her as a child. We had only recently renewed our acquaintance." He looked down at the dark patterned rug as they waited for the elevator. "Am I to understand that she is dead?"

"Yes," Margaret said. The archduke sighed.

When they reached the street, Archduke Niklas nodded graciously to a tall black youth leaning against a low wall beside the building's front door.

"Good evening, Marcus," he said.

"Yo, sir." Another level of society responded appropriately to the aura of position and dignity.

"He delivers food from Navets Nouveaux," the archduke explained. "Emma likes . . . liked him."

"Don't think about it," Margaret said soothingly. De Vere

detoured to a police cruiser double-parked in the street and spoke to a uniformed officer, while Margaret guided the archduke to De Vere's unmarked car.

They rode in silence across town through Central Park and yet farther west, then uptown to a looming gray stone apartment building that perched over a strip of park along the Hudson River. Margaret escorted the old man to the massive doorway of the building.

"You'll be all right?" she said. "Shall I ring you tomorrow?"

"I am not now on the telephone," he said. "Perhaps you could come to call. My place is not what I would like to receive visitors, since I am not able to have the servants I once did. Yes, I would be grateful if you called in the afternoon." Margaret felt his frail hand gently squeeze her arm. "And your young man, if he would care to come."

"I think he might," Margaret said. But she had someone more manageable than De Vere in mind.

Chapter 4

*T*he next morning, Margaret did not rise early, but stared at the ceiling with the blankets tucked under her chin and reviewed a conversational passage between her and De Vere as they drove away from the archduke's building.

> DE VERE: *I won't allow you to become further involved.*
> MARGARET (testy): *Allow? I don't understand you.*
> DE VERE: *You do. As soon as I was passed the word that you were at that woman's place . . .*
> MARGARET (with some disbelief): *The word was passed? About me?*
> DE VERE: *They said a call had come in reporting a murder. The caller said that Lady Margaret Priam was guarding the body, so naturally . . .*
> MARGARET: *Naturally. You flew to my side. I believe I merely suggested that someone ought to call the police. How curious. I suppose you are taken up with your police work for the rest of the night.*
> DE VERE: *I am. Sorry. Promise me that you will tell Russo the facts as you know them, and not delve further into what happened to this dead woman.*
> MARGARET (affronted): *I certainly am not interested in what happened to Emma.*
> DE VERE: *My dear Margaret, that is such an untruth that even my sainted mother wouldn't hesitate to tell you so.*

27

MARGARET (as though distracted from murder by the mention of De Vere's mother): *I must call your mother. We haven't spoken in ages.*

Margaret had long ago realized that De Vere's concerns about her safety were colored by a strong masculine belief that he knew what was best, and could not be moved. Thus she did not add her next thought, "What do you suppose Emma was really up to?"

She thought about it again as she lay drowsing in her bed. Then she threw off her blankets and sat up. Of course Emma had been up to something, and it was something more than extracting a few much-needed dollars from an ostensibly naive man, or acquiring a jeweled trinket, or caging a free airline ticket to prosperous hunting grounds.

Who would know? Her chum Marie d'Avalon? Perhaps, but Marie was as slippery as Dianne Stark's bias-cut satin gown. If Emma and the archduke were close of late, he might know something, even if the poor old man might not understand what it was about.

Margaret hated to rouse Paul Castrocani so early on a Saturday morning, but crime does not allow for sleeping in.

"Yes?" A half-awake Paul answered on the fifth ring.

"It's Margaret. Paul, I want you to accompany me to see an old friend today. Please say yes without an argument."

"Conditionally. When? I was out dancing until dawn. And who?"

"He's an archduke," Margaret said. "Very charming, and very, very old. He has agreed to receive us this afternoon."

"Hmm." Prince Paul Castrocani was thinking. "There are few archdukes about. Perhaps a Hapsburg or two, and a Romanov, or are they grand dukes? Not currently reigning, I take it, or about to ascend a throne?"

"Paul," Margaret said, "do not deny an old man his fantasy. Do it for me."

"Does it have anything to do with that murder you're mixed up in?"

"You heard? Have you been talking to De Vere?"

"Not at all. I only know what I read in the papers I bought

on the way home. 'Titled Englishwoman . . . Victim of Forced Entry . . . Violent Death.' The usual.''

"Ha!" Margaret said. "Seldom forced. Go on."

She heard the rustle of papers over the phone. Paul read slowly, " 'Among the guests at the fashionable party where the body was discovered were high-fashion designer Kendall Smith, whose forthcoming book *Feathers and Fashion Through History* will be honored with a prepublication party hosted by Belinda Hope, wife of . . .' and so forth. It mentions you—'Lady Margaret Priam, whose brother the earl of . . .' ''

"Enough," Margaret said. "Which witch decided to do a little self-promotion? Kendall? Belinda? Oh, it doesn't matter. The archduke was there, a friend of the victim. I promised I'd call on him today. He'd appreciate a titled gentleman like you in attendance."

Margaret thought she heard a resigned sigh. "It won't cause you a bit of trouble, Paul. We'll stop by at about four, stay for half an hour, and then we'll retire to some expensive spot for high tea. You'll be home in time to dress for an evening of fun with your latest lady."

In the end, in order to terminate the phone call and return to sleep, Paul agreed.

Margaret too retreated again under her blankets. This time she closed her eyes and summoned up the picture of Emma's bedroom and bath, and tried not to see the horrible face on the floor.

The emptiness of the bedroom. Emma was not the type to pare her lifestyle to the bone. Therefore she had removed her belongings, perhaps quite recently.

The dress. Kenny Smith charged at least two thousand for his designer gowns, but there was the matter of the hem. If Emma had somehow extracted it directly from him, it would not have been necessary for her to take up the hem, shoddily or otherwise. Kenny had seamstresses. Borrowed then—if not from Kendall's salon, then from whom?

She saw the smudge of eye shadow on the gown, the silver slippers with their perilous heels, the old bathrobe, the glamorous undergarments. The flashy lingerie in the drawer, the nearly empty closets.

Forced entry? A robber? Impossible . . .

Margaret leapt from her cozy bed, inspired by an interesting thought. She splashed through her shower and raced through her makeup and dressing—black of course, since there was no telling whether she'd get back to her apartment before the visit to the archduke. The Edwardian diamond brooch inherited from her grandmother was not exactly right for daytime wear, but quite right for Archduke Niklas.

She remembered to ring Bedros Kasparian at his Madison Avenue Oriental antique shop to beg off work.

"Something critical has come up," she said when he answered.

"Ah. Critical." She imagined Kasparian pacing the fine Chinese silk rug on his showroom floor, trailing the long phone cord behind him. "And it would relate to what I have just been reading in the newspapers? A murder? Tsk."

Now Margaret could imagine him shaking his round, bald head with its brave fringe of white. Kasparian would be nearly as old as the archduke, but was rather more vigorous.

"It happened long before I arrived at a little drinks party Emma Ross invited me to."

"Please, I understand. Saturdays are slow, and in any case, I have a customer coming to view my Persian miniatures. He takes hours to decide, and in the end, I will refuse to sell them."

"Thank you," Margaret said. "You are an angel. Oh yes, are you acquainted with one Archduke Niklas, country of origin unknown?"

"I know the name," Kasparian said cautiously. "I don't believe I ever heard that he could afford my prices. Poppy Dill would have the particulars of his life stored away."

"I thought of Poppy," Margaret said, "but I was afraid she'd be cross with me for not ringing her up immediately when the body was discovered."

Poppy Dill, although reclusive, was remarkably knowledgeable about everything that had to do with prominent society names (even if somewhat suspect, like Emma's), the better to produce her daily newspaper society column, "Social Scene."

"Miss Dill will want to hear anything you have to say," Kasparian said, "even if it is too late to make the early editions."

"I'll be at the shop at first light on Monday," Margaret said.

"I expect it will be Tuesday if you are busy gathering clues," he said. "You'll arrive with murderer in hand?"

"Of course not," Margaret said sweetly. "The police will handle all that. It was one of the lower orders—forced entry, robbery, murder."

"If you say so, my dear," Kasparian said. "My best regards to De Vere, if he still speaks to you in view of this new murder."

Margaret had already opened her apartment door to depart when the telephone rang. She hesitated, then picked up before the answering machine whirred into action.

"Lady Margaret? This is Tina Corrado."

"Indeed," was all Margaret could think to say.

"Mr. Dalton wonders if you would be free this evening for dinner, to discuss some business matters. He apologizes for not calling personally, but he is talking to the authorities about Lady Ross's death."

"Business matters?" Margaret said to give herself time to think.

It seemed impossible to her that Yale Dalton would choose murder as a means of dismissing a public relations manager who had failed him, but one could not be too careful nowadays. On the other hand, if Emma had been up to something more with Yale than making a few profitable introductions, he might be persuaded to let slip what he knew as the silverware gleamed in the candlelight. Temptation to know overcame Margaret's better judgment.

"He needs some advice, now that Lady Ross is dead," Tina said. "She was rather involved in his affairs."

"Ah," Margaret said. Yale Dalton might have marked her as an Emma substitute, whether for making his way into the upper reaches of New York life or something more. "To-night? Let me see." She tried to keep Saturday nights open for De Vere in case he had time from his work. Then the need to know what Emma had been up to won out. "I could arrange to be free," she said finally. "But I doubt that I can be of any help to him."

"Mr. Dalton will pick you up at eight," Tina said. "Good-bye." Superefficient Tina might be, but not exactly overflowing with warmth.

Margaret tried to recall the name of the food shop the arch-duke had mentioned as they left Emma's building. The black delivery boy's name was Marcus, that she did recall. The shop could not be too difficult to locate. It would be within a few blocks north or south of the cross street where Emma resided, on Lexington or Third Avenues, just possibly on Second. In any case, not too distant from her own apartment and a nice morning walk on a fairly warm autumn day.

When she saw Navets Nouveaux on Third Avenue, she knew she had found what she was looking for.

The seriously white shop was crowded with young Upper Eastsiders collecting *potages* and *salades*, *baguettes* and *fromages* for *intime* Saturday brunches, washed down with decent blanc de blancs. The aroma of freshly ground coffees and crusty hot breads mingled with the scents of Obsession, Eternity, and something that might be Uninhibited.

The harassed counter girl waved Margaret to the back of the shop, where a middle-aged man with bushy brows and curly black hair was fawning over an elegantly casual young couple who were trying to decide between a tarte and a torte.

"Madame?" the man said, when the couple had departed with both tarte and torte. He had a heavy French accent, and with his long white apron looked like the *boulanger* in some provincial French village.

Margaret decided to speak French, the happy result of her schooling in Switzerland. "I am seeking the boy who delivers for your shop," she said. "Marcus."

The man's face grew purplish with Gallic rage. "He is gone. I put him out. An assassin, working at Navets Nouveaux! The shame of it! The police have him, for all I know. And if not, then the Devil."

"Do you know where he lives?"

"I know nothing of this boy."

"But he worked here for some time."

The man looked down, looked up, and admitted it finally. "He claims he did not commit any crime—except that he accepted a check from Madame Lady Ross in payment for the delivery. I sent him back to collect good hard cash from that one. No checks."

"And did he return with the cash?"

"Alas, Madame, he did not. He claims that the lady had been found dead and the police were there. Then . . ." The man shrugged. "The police decided that he was suspected in this death. The shame! And the check will not be good, as is usual."

"Is it possible that Marcus did this crime?"

The man shrugged again, softening. "Marcus did not cause me any trouble. A good worker, but you never know. The temptations, the money, the goods stolen to pay for illicit pleasures . . ."

"But not necessarily murder," Margaret said. "Come, now, monsieur, you must know where he lives. I may be able to help him out of his trouble. As you say, he is not a bad boy. . . ."

"There is an address for his mother," the man said reluctantly. He disappeared into a back room, while Margaret eavesdropped on two young things peering into the display case near her.

"Thank goodness," one said, "they've finally managed to stem the framboise tide. There was getting to be just *too* much raspberry this and raspberry that for the world to retain its proper perspective."

"You know," the other said, "I *hate* to confess it, but I'm *really* tired of goat cheese. . . ."

"Here," the man said, and offered a slip of paper to Margaret. "I do not wish Marcus ill. But what could I do? I have a reputation . . . my customers, what would they think?"

"I understand," Margaret said. "Many thanks."

Outside the shop, Margaret looked at the paper. She was not familiar with Flatbush, although she understood that it was a rather long trip to the depths of Brooklyn. Perhaps there was some way to telephone, although no number was given. She put the paper carefully into her bag and headed for her next stop: Poppy Dill.

"Miss Dill is *out*?" Margaret was shocked. Poppy Dill never left her apartment except under the greatest compulsion. Margaret believed that the last recorded time was a visit of the Princess of Wales to New York.

"Yes, ma'am," the doorman said. "It was quite a surprise to me too. Big white limousine drives up to the door, here comes Miss Dill all dressed up, the chauffeur opens the car door, and off they go."

"I am speechless," Margaret said. "Was there an indication of when she will return? No, wait. I think I know. The wedding."

"Ma'am?" The doorman was puzzled.

"Not Miss Dill's wedding. The Zander wedding. You know, that fabulously rich Thom Zander who left his wife to run off with Paula Craft who left *her* husband who wasn't so rich but very nice, and now that they're both divorced—they're getting married today. Poppy would never miss that."

"I see," the doorman said, but obviously didn't read Poppy Dill's column regularly enough to follow closely the saga of the Zander-Craft scandal.

"I'll just catch a cab over to the Plaza," Margaret said. "And try to track Miss Dill down after the ceremony." Margaret eschewed the particular *nouveau riche* circle in which the Zanders and Crafts traveled, so had not been one of the lucky hundreds who were descending upon the Plaza Hotel to witness the forging of the momentous union.

"You want to get out here, lady?" The cab driver was glumly watching the green lights change to red and back on Fifth Avenue as no traffic moved. "There must be some rock star at the Plaza or something."

A mass of people milled around the Pulitzer Fountain in

front of the Plaza Hotel, the avid followers of the New York social scene who had come out to see the rich and the very rich arrive to witness the nuptials of the obscenely rich.

"There's an important wedding today," Margaret said.

"Oh, yeah?" The cab driver was mildly interested. "It must be some kind of king to draw that crowd."

"Only commonplace rich people, I'm afraid," Margaret said, "but I am reminded of the root causes of the French Revolution. . . ."

She departed the cab and made her way across Fifth to the hotel.

"They let that Wall Street man, the one who stole forty million dollars, out of jail so he could come to this," said one of the throng within Margaret's hearing.

"I hope he brought a nice gift," said his companion. "Somebody said Cher was supposed to be here."

Margaret headed toward the Central Park South side of the Plaza, where she found many fine and distinguished limousines triple parked, blithely obstructing traffic in a manner that was beginning to create total gridlock throughout the city. There were two white limos. The chauffeur of the first she approached rolled down a smoked window and advised her of the name of the owner: the widow of a deposed head of state, not infrequently referred to as a dictator and looter of his country's treasury. Margaret spoke to the driver of the second, who put aside his *Daily News*, and looked her up and down.

"Is this Miss Dill's car?"

"Yes, ma'am," the driver said.

"Lovely," Margaret said. "I'm meeting her."

"Yeah, but I can't let you wait in the car. . . ."

"Naturally not," Margaret said graciously. "As long as I've found the right car, I'll just hover about, shall I?"

"It won't be long," the driver said. "She's coming right out that door after the ceremony, so I can get her home and pick up the boss and the wife."

"And they would be?"

The driver looked at her suspiciously. "Mr. and Mrs. Norman Hope."

"Remarkable," Margaret said. "I saw Norman and Belinda only last evening. I had no idea they would be invited to the Zander wedding." Nor did Margaret have any idea that the Hopes could afford the extremely heavy expense of owning their own limousine.

The driver shrugged. "They aren't exactly at this wedding. They just asked to be picked up here so people would think they were invited. And he's not exactly my boss. I mean, this is my car, I have a limo service, but I do Norm a favor now and then for a cut-rate price. We grew up in the same old neighborhood."

"How convenient," Margaret said. "Ah, look. The deed has been done, and here's Miss Dill."

Poppy Dill emerged from the revolving doors of the Plaza, supported across the crimson carpeting by two young uniformed employees. Considering her advanced age, she looked quite chic.

"How brave of you to come out for the wedding, Poppy," Margaret said. "And what a lovely dress."

"Mainbocher made it especially for me when he was a mere boy," Poppy said. "It is a relief to see you, Margaret. These social things are so nerve-wracking. But I do agree that Ivana has done a wonderful job fixing up the old Plaza."

She was inserted into the limousine with the help of Margaret and the Plaza doormen. Margaret sank into the luxurious backseat beside her.

"They are well and truly married, although I won't predict for how long. And the late—the former—Mrs. Zander got such a wonderful divorce settlement, so everyone is happy."

"And rich," Margaret said. "Shall we hurry back to your place? I have some things to ask you."

"Home," Poppy said grandly to her borrowed chauffeur, and they headed back to the safe and civilized East Side.

Chapter 5

"*All right,*" Poppy said when she had changed into her favorite lacy peignoir and was seated comfortably in a big armchair in her boudoir cum office, "tell me all about it."

"It?"

"Emma Ross's murder. I should be very, very angry with you. I had to read about it in the papers, and then I had to endure an *endless* phone call from Belinda Hope, who certainly got everything wrong. She's almost more trouble than she's worth."

"You're close to Belinda?" Margaret asked.

Poppy dismissed the Hopes with a wave of her hand. "Kenny Smith has this book he's written about feathers or some such nonsense. Belinda was persuaded to create a charity party for the publication. Emma had a hand in the persuading. She was helping Kenny with his astonishing self-promotion for a time. You must have heard about his new ready-to-wear line. The only organization that was on the lookout for a charity thing has something to do with preserving wildlife. I told Belinda that slaughtering birds for the sake of fashion did not serve the best interests of wildlife, but she wouldn't listen. In any case, I promised Kenny to help promote it in my column, but that entails a *faux* friendship with that woman, until it comes off."

"And the convenient loan of the putative Hope limousine."

"Can you imagine the lengths some people go to to appear far wealthier than they are?" Poppy beamed contentedly. A free limo is after all a free limo. She rearranged her frock about her feet, and Margaret imagined that Kenny Smith had provided a few expensive (but free) peignoirs to bolster Poppy's good will.

"I can easily measure the lengths," Margaret said. "And I did come round to ask about the Hopes, and Emma and her friend, Archduke Niklas."

Poppy pondered. "Nicky was quite naughty for a good part of this century, you know. People forget, but not I. He was very handsome as a young man. I used to meet him abroad from time to time years ago."

"But he's not a real archduke, I take it."

"Well, probably not. But certainly he's vaguely related to one of those little kings who didn't manage to hold the pieces together after the First World War. Was it Bulgaria? Serbia? Montenegro? My memory isn't what it was."

Margaret knew that wasn't true. Poppy remembered everything.

"Tell me more about naughty Nicky."

"Nothing special. He was part of that wild life in Paris and the Riviera and places like that between the wars. I seem to recall that Gertrude Stein loathed him, Picasso tolerated him, and Hemingway had a crush on him. But mostly he enjoyed well-planned liaisons with well-heeled ladies who weren't much bothered by the Depression. Noble heroics in the Second World War—'for the sake of the homeland' which hadn't existed per se for decades. If he wants to call himself archduke, more power to him." ·

"That's all? The woods are full of such grand old deceivers. Does he have money at all?"

"He scrapes by, conferring orders and titles on persons who can afford his price. Nice enough little trinkets, clusters of this and that on red ribbons. He even gave me one for nothing, because I didn't print a story about a tiny contretemps that occurred in his later years. The lady was rather older than he, if you can believe it. I haven't laid eyes on him in years. I always thought he should have been clever enough to have laid something by for his old age, but perhaps he was unlucky. There was . . ." Poppy stopped. "I shouldn't gossip," she said.

"But you *must*," Margaret said, exasperated. If Poppy shouldn't gossip, then the entire world must be silent.

"Well . . . Has Marie d'Avalon ever spoken to you of him?"

"Marie? About the archduke? No, but we aren't exactly intimates. You know she found Emma's body."

"Really? How typical of her to be in the middle of a mess."

"But what did you mean about Marie and Archduke Niklas?"

"What I do know to be absolutely a fact is that years ago, back in the thirties, one of Niklas's girlfriends was a too sweet, too rich American girl. What is absolute *rumor* . . . that is, people have said . . . that there was a daughter. . . ."

"People? What sort of people?"

"It was Marie actually. She implied . . . hmmm . . . close ties?"

"Oh Poppy, that's absurd. That would mean Marie was not only suggesting she was the archduke's daughter, but confessing that she was over fifty!"

"I never believed it myself. She hates to remember that she's an American pure and simple, in a manner of speaking. I'm sure it could be determined that the man her mother eventually married was responsible for Marie. But she did once suggest some beneficial financial aspect to being related to Niklas. She didn't care for that blossoming relationship between him and Emma. I hate to think she murdered Emma over the remnants of doubtful crown jewels."

"And what was Emma Ross to him?" Margaret was thinking that it was very likely that the archduke might have understood quite well what Emma was up to.

"Birds of a feather, don't you think? Opportunistic, and with a common taste for devising fanciful titles with no basis in reality. Lady Ross, indeed." Poppy shrugged. "I never found out where the name came from. Not a soul in England ever heard of her or anybody named Ross she might have married. Weren't you and she buddies back when you'd just arrived in New York?''

"I knew her," Margaret said. "I never probed too deeply about how she came to be Lady Ross. We went about a bit for a time, but she was . . ." Margaret hesitated. "She was rather an embarrassment."

"A joke," Poppy said, "but only half a fool. Perhaps she was lonely, and she and the archduke could pretend together. Perhaps he was a bit in love with her, his last romantic gasp. And now she's dead." Poppy shook her head. "She must have been up to something."

"Exactly what I thought," Margaret said. "The police think someone forced his way in with robbery in mind and killed her. A delivery boy."

"Much more likely someone like Norman Hope. Or Belinda," Poppy said. She leaned forward confidentially. "I don't know if you ever heard this, but when Norman was getting started in the money business, he and our Emma were alleged to have been rather intimate. Belinda pretended she didn't know, but of course she did. Wives do. Belinda has been making so much noise lately about Norman's big deals that I think she's setting him up for an expensive divorce. But I never heed talk of big deals until there's something to show for it." Poppy meant a limo truly one's own, the purchase of an apartment so grand that it was worth column space, an estate in the country, and other extravagances that suggested assets in quantity.

"This is more than I wanted to know," Margaret said. "I don't suppose you know anything of a Yale Dalton?"

Poppy looked at her blankly, then shook her head. If Poppy didn't know of him, he was not worth knowing.

"He was at Emma's party. She was doing public relations for him."

Poppy raised an eyebrow.

Margaret laughed. "Exactly my thought. But there was more than publicity involved. Some sort of scheme is afoot, and I'll discover it when I dine with Dalton tonight."

"He's not the murderer, is he?"

Margaret shrugged. "I don't know. He could have been there ahead of everyone to do the foul deed. Poppy, I have a favor to ask. Not a big one," she added quickly. Poppy kept close track of the size of favors given and received. "I was wondering if your connections at the newspaper could obtain a telephone number attached to an address."

"Surely your De Vere and his New York Police Department could manage that," Poppy said.

"I'd rather he didn't know," Margaret said.

"Ha! Tracking down the murderer on your own! I've given you a load of suspects."

"Oh, no," Margaret said. "I promised De Vere I'd keep out."

"Have it your way," Poppy said. "Yes, there's somebody at the paper who could manage it."

"Good." Margaret gave Poppy the address in Brooklyn that was allegedly the home of Marcus's mother.

"It may take a while," Poppy said. "I'll call you if my person comes up with anything. You know, I'm always surprised to discover that some people actually don't have telephones. I'm not sure what the situation is in Brooklyn."

"The old archduke seems not to have a telephone, but I imagine modern civilization has reached Flatbush," Margaret said, "although perhaps not as visibly as in Manhattan."

"You are so witty, Margaret," Poppy said. "Look now." She opened a drawer and extracted a handful of heavy cream envelopes, all beautifully addressed in calligraphic handwriting. "I certainly am not going to attend any of these parties I've been invited to. Why don't you take De Vere to one or two?"

"De Vere has stated that he will never again consent to attend an affair where the per capita income is equal to or higher than that of Kuwait," Margaret said. "Or was it Brunei?"

"It must have been Brunei," Poppy said. "The sultan is

a dear boy and his country does very well in terms of per capita income.''

Margaret took the invitations, just in case.

Kendall Smith had his showroom and offices in the fashionable reaches of Madison Avenue, not far from Kasparian's antique shop. The big guns of fashion clustered together farther downtown on Seventh Avenue, but Kendall marched to his own tin drum. Margaret thought she might catch him in on a Saturday afternoon, since a great many socially active women always waited until the last minute to pick up a pricey gown.

The showroom was on the second floor of a four-story building. In its tall windows overlooking the avenue stood two faceless, attenuated mannequins in glamorous Kendall frocks. Lots of gold and sequins this year—and yes, plenty of feathers. Margaret could see a gaunt model slinking across the room to show off a hot number in Kenny's trademark bloodred to a customer.

"By appointment only," said a melodious voice when Margaret rang the bell at the ground floor entrance.

"Would you tell Mr. Smith that Lady Margaret Priam wishes to speak to him?"

There was a click as the voice turned off the intercom. Then, after a few seconds, the door buzzed and Margaret pushed it open. The narrow staircase to the second floor was carpeted with—could it be?—dark green velvet. The banister was gleaming brass. The floor of the tiny foyer at the top was green marble (surely not malachite) inlaid with colored stones in an intricate floral pattern. Margaret entered the showroom and received a brief, bored glance from a woman lounging on a sofa watching the model fling her draperies around. Kendall's customer had hair that wouldn't bow to a tornado and a maquillage that could withstand a blizzard.

"This way, please," said the lovely voice, which was attached to a rather plain young woman with hair cropped to the skull at back and sides. "Mr. Smith is terribly busy, but he'll make a bit of time for you, Lady Margaret."

"How very kind of him," Margaret murmured. The

woman on the sofa looked sharply at Margaret at the mention of her title.

Kendall Smith sat on the floor of his office surrounded by bolts of glimmering, shimmering fabrics, piles of swatches, a stack of sketchbooks, and an open box of watercolors. He was wearing jeans and a denim work shirt, and was holding a large sketch of a ball gown at arm's length.

"Here is Lady Margaret," the girl said. "She has promised not to take too much of your time." She closed the door firmly behind her.

"I promised no such thing," Margaret said, "which is not to say that I won't be brief."

"Please, your ladyship, take as much time as you want," Kendall said grandly. "Louise is too protective, and these things are simply dreadful. I can't bear to look at them one more minute. Too much work for too little return. I doubt that Oscar and Carolina and Donna put in the hours that I do, and look at them, rich and famous." Kendall flung the sketches aside and popped to his feet. He stretched to kiss Margaret on both cheeks. "After all, Maggie dear, we're almost partners in crime after last night. Come along, sit down here and gossip. Who do you suppose did poor Emma in?" He looked at her eagerly for an answer, but Margaret could only shrug. "Such a shock to my system, and then all that silly stuff in the papers," he said.

Margaret was amused. "Surely any mention of *Feathers and Fashion* is to your benefit."

"Oh that. Somebody asked, so I told them. I do find it useful to keep putting my name before the public. You *are* coming to my little publication party, aren't you? No? But you must! It's masquerade. Wear something feathery, or only a pretty mask if you wish. I'm taking the opportunity to make the big announcement about my new line—the ready-to-wear label. I'm simply thrilled about that, real profits at last. I'm doing everything: evening wear, resort wear, daytime. Probably sportswear at some point, and I see fabulous accessories down the road. I've just about decided to leave the sunglasses to St. Laurent, and the jeans to Lauren. . . ."

"It sounds highly ambitious," Margaret said.

"It *is*! But it's the only way. One-of-a kind designer dresses have such a limited market. I think it was Emma who gave me the idea: clothes for Everywoman. She couldn't afford my prices, and she didn't look right in my couture designs. I believe it was Cecil Beaton who said you could lead a woman to a Dior dress, but how she'd look in it was another matter. Still holds true. Poor Emma was looking forward to my party. I even promised her a gorgeous little costume."

"Speaking of costumes, there's something curious you might be able to explain," Margaret said. "Emma was planning to wear one of your dresses last night. A sort of rose-colored chiffon thing, quite decolleté, a long sweeping skirt, and that fabulous embroidery you use so well. Very pretty, needless to say."

Kendall took off his round wire-rimmed spectacles and polished them carefully. "Curious, as you say," he said. "If you're asking whether Emma obtained such a garment from me, the answer is definitely not. If you're asking who did buy the dress, the answer is Marie d'Avalon. The *soi-disant* comtesse can't afford me either, but happily she always has great and good friends who can. But Emma in that dress? She was yards shorter than Marie. She couldn't possibly have worn that dress."

"She'd taken it up at the hem," Margaret said. "And not skillfully."

"Well!" Kendall began to pace. "I am shocked. That would ruin the line. I am *definitely* glad she did not live to wear it. I have a reputation, and *that* depends heavily on the people who wear my clothes. She would have looked like . . . like a rose-colored dumpling. It would have been a disaster." Kendall kicked a bolt of orange crepe de chine and paced some more. He seemed very put out.

"How do you suppose Marie came to lend it to her?"

"Emma had a gift for extracting gifts, making promises, manipulating people."

"She could be amusing, and that facade of amiable stupidity left one defenseless. And she was always so hopeful, in spite of evidence to the contrary." Margaret felt obliged to defend Emma.

"Don't get sentimental about Lady Ross," Kendall said. "True she did a bit of useful work for me, and I shall notice that she's not about rattling on about her silly plans and schemes, but I really can't remember now why we put up with her."

"I'm not," Margaret said. "But I do wonder what she was up to, and why she got herself strangled for her troubles."

"It was robbery. The papers said so, although there were people who must have felt like throttling her."

"I don't know what to think," Margaret said, "but I'm sure the police will straighten things out. I was simply curious about the dress. It was definitely Marie's?'

"Absolutely," Kendall said.

"Any idea about who paid for it?"

"Marie didn't say. She came in one day, looked at several things, and picked that one out. She came back the next day with cash, and told me how fabulous she thought the gown was, and she simply had to own it. Perhaps Marie murdered Emma when she saw what she had done to my creation."

"A bit extreme, don't you think?"

"I don't know about that," Kendall said airily. "Women have been known to say they'd kill for one of my gowns."

Chapter 6

Although Comtesse Marie d'Avalon tried not to publicize the fact that she lived in a smallish studio apartment in a high rise in the Thirties rather than in palatial luxury, Margaret knew. She also knew that Marie would not welcome a spontaneous visitor. Yet it seemed relatively important to clear up the tale of the dress and the rumors about the woman's alleged kinship with the poor old archduke. The telephone, Margaret thought, might suffice, so she returned to her own apartment before visiting the archduke. A call to Marie would have to substitute for looking her in the eye.

When Margaret opened her apartment door, she saw that the light on the answering machine signified calls on the tape. She hoped Paul wasn't backing out while De Vere found himself free for the evening.

It was only half bad. Unless she heard otherwise, Paul would meet her in front of her building at three-thirty. That was all right. De Vere wanted to meet for dinner before he had to return to the complicated paperwork that a current case entailed—nefarious activities that sported white collars. He preferred to be on the streets pursuing criminals who merely aspired to a BMW in every garage and a condo in the Bahamas, rather than sitting in an office tracing the illegal acts of those who already possessed everything and wanted more, much more.

Here was a dilemma: to call De Vere and explain that she was otherwise engaged, or not to call until much later—too late for dinner—and explain that she had only just gotten in. In neither case would either of them be happy. Margaret was never certain if she was tied irrevocably to De Vere. They didn't seem able to stay apart for long. Periodically there were flashes of intimacy that promised a mutual future, and then cooled in the light of their very different lifestyles. They were both a bit too independent for conventional bonds—but Margaret still tended to feel guilty when she did things De Vere strongly disapproved of.

She bravely decided to call De Vere, tell him something was up, and not tell him that it was Yale Dalton. Her modest reward for being brave was learning that De Vere was away from his desk.

"Oh, dear," she said, hoping the relief in her voice wasn't obvious. "I am returning his call, but I can't be reached until very late." She was fleetingly ashamed of this cowardly escape.

There was a message from Russo, the detective who was in charge of Emma's murder. He wished to speak to her on Monday.

Then a call came from Poppy. "I remembered something else about Marie's mother," Poppy said. "Her family was in oil and ranches and the like, like Paul's mother, except Marie's family lost its money, and that will never happen to Carolyn Sue. Naturally Marie had to become a fortune hunter, and not a good one at that. I thought you'd like to know."

"Indeed I do," Margaret said.

"Oh, yes," Poppy went on, "here's a phone number in Brooklyn that might be the one you wanted. And tell me *everything*!"

Margaret called Brooklyn. The woman who answered did not quite admit that she knew anyone named Marcus, and the male voice who next spoke didn't quite admit that he was Marcus.

"I'd like to meet with Marcus," Margaret said. "It could be to his advantage. It's about Lady Ross and the murder."

"Hey, man, he don't want to get in more trouble." Then, proudly, "He got a lawyer."

"Good, but I think I could help get him out of trouble," Margaret said. In the end, the male voice who might or might not have been Marcus said that Marcus would appear tomorrow at a location named by Margaret at a time she mentioned, for the consideration she suggested. Then she dialed Marie.

Marie d'Avalon, whatever her antecedents, had affected a continental accent linked to no specific language ever since she was briefly wed to the comte who probably thought she was rich, while she believed the same of him. Bad luck to both.

"Daaarrrling, I am devastated. I can barely speak. To think that I came upon that horrrrible sight, even if it was a woman I scarcely knew. The gendarmes with their questions—what did I see? What did I notice? What did I touch? I touch nothing, I see nothing except this woman lying on the floor. . . ."

"Marie, I . . ."

"You cannot imagine the horrror, the sight of her. A little party I would stop at for so short a time, nothing to speak of, no one of importance. I come as a favor to this woman, and you see what she does to me."

A spot of trouble in life was apparently far more significant to Marie than the terminal trouble represented by Emma's death.

"Marie!" Margaret spoke quite sharply as Marie took a breath to continue. "I rang to see how you were after your ordeal," Margaret said soothingly, "and to ask whether you'll have any difficulty retrieving the dress you loaned to Emma."

"Drrrress? I do not loan my dresses," Marie said grandly.

"Your new Kendall Smith gown," Margaret said. "The one Emma had to take up the hem on. You must have noticed. . . ." Perhaps Marie had been so disturbed at noticing it that she had done away with Emma. Or perhaps she had been so taken up with her discovery of Emma not to have noticed the crude hem at all.

"The hem taken up? Impossible."

"I might have been mistaken," Margaret said, although she was not. "She was quite a bit shorter than you."

"That would be an outrage, to trifle with a Kendall." Marie sounded seriously affronted. "If I had loaned such a gown, I would naturally expect to have it returned to me. I have been assured . . . That is to say, one assumes that if one loaned a very expensive dress, it would be returned promptly."

"It could be evidence, locked away for months," Margaret said, feeling slightly malicious. "The police are peculiar that way."

"What?" Marie sounded distracted, as though picturing her multi-thousand-dollar gown forever incarcerated as a piece of evidence in a murder.

"It could be months," Margaret said. "Have you spoken to Archduke Niklas since the murder?"

"Why would I do that? A senile old man, whom nobody wants to know."

"Ah, I understood that you and he were related—through your former husband perhaps? Or your mother?"

"What do you know of that? I have *never* claimed . . . these miserable women who tittle and tattle all day long . . . I deny . . ."

"We ought to have lunch one day," Margaret said sweetly. "Very soon. Oh, yes—how well do you know Emma's friend Yale Dalton?"

"Why do you ask that?" Marie sounded entirely put out now.

"I don't know much about him, but since you and Emma were so close . . . He is taking me to dinner this evening."

There was silence on the other end of the line.

"Marie? Are you there?"

"Someone rang from downstairs. I must go, there is a visitor. I will ring you soon. Yes, we must sit and talk."

Marie slammed down the receiver. Pity her poor visitor. With the thought uppermost that it might be ages before she reacquired her Kendall, crude hem and all, Marie was not likely to be pleasant company.

Margaret sat at her dressing table to repair her makeup and consider Marie as a suspect.

Why had Marie lied—tried to lie—about the dress? Kendall was hot, but he certainly hadn't set the entire world aflame. He wasn't de la Renta or Adolfo or Valentino. Surely it was more a matter of denying her friendship with the victim. And why had she denied her claims to the archduke? If Poppy knew the tale she was telling, surely everyone knew. Or perhaps it was merely Marie's first instinct to lie.

Margaret was waiting downstairs when Paul arrived. He arrived not on foot or by cab, but in a low-slung gleaming black sports car, with a throbbing engine that hinted at three-digit speeds. Margaret's doorman rushed to open the passenger door for her, then stood back to admire the car.

"What on earth is this?" Margaret said as she settled back into the curved bucket seat upholstered with pliant soft black leather.

Paul's dark eyes were aglow, and he looked like a six-year-old who'd been presented with his first bicycle. "It is a little gift from my mother," Paul said. "It may be that she has struck oil again."

"Paul, it's a Ferrari! Never mind how much it cost, you will have to hire a permanent guardian to keep it from being stolen from the streets of Manhattan in the next ten minutes."

"I know," Paul said sadly, and raced the engine. "I know. But," he added cheerfully, "she is insured and I am madly in love with her."

The trip to the archduke in a new Ferrari with an infatuated Italian prince at the wheel was a unique experience. The city streets were viewed from close to the ground, and the covetous looks from pedestrians waiting at street lights were unsettling. One didn't like being directly involved with New Yorkers' lust for virtually unattainable material goods.

"Does De Vere know about this?" Margaret asked as they zoomed under the culverts of Central Park to the West Side. De Vere had long shared Paul's Chelsea duplex apartment, owned by Paul's mother and given to the ever-impecunious

Paul rent-free. De Vere's rent came to Paul as a much-needed source of extra income. The salary at United National Bank & Trust where he worked barely paid for his lifestyle peripherals. De Vere and Paul kept separate hours and separate phones, indeed nearly separate floors, so their lives seldom intersected.

"I have not seen him in some days," Paul said. "A note did not seem appropriate. The drama lies in viewing this angel with the eyes."

"He will disapprove," Margaret said, and held on as Paul swooped out of the park onto Central Park West. He braked for a red light and grinned. He was such a handsome young man with his strong features and lustrous dark hair that it was a pity he only fell in love with unattainable heiresses who seldom got to enjoy his genuine good-heartedness. Now, of course, he loved his Ferrari, which Margaret knew would escape him sooner or later.

"De Vere will love her too," Paul said. "Trust me. I know how a man feels."

Paul managed to find a spot for his car close to the door of the archduke's gray granite apartment building, but Margaret sensed that he was nervous.

"Come along," she said. "It's not a bad neighborhood."

"No neighborhood is safe," Paul said gloomily. "I should not leave her this way."

"What do you do in your neighborhood? Chelsea is rather crime-prone, is it not?"

"I put her in a garage," Paul said, "and I have informed the attendants that if anything happens to her, my uncle the Mafia godfather of all of Sicily will see them dismembered."

"You aren't Sicilian," Margaret said. "You have no such uncle."

"They do not know that," Paul said. "I will stay but a few moments."

The hall of the looming building had seen its original grandeur pass. There were vestiges of fine architectural touches, but the multiple names on the buzzers indicated that the place had become a haven for Columbia University graduate students sharing high drafty rooms with as many bodies as could comfortably fit in order to reduce each share of the rent to the lowest amount. Only the card bearing the word NIKLAS stood alone. Margaret admired the confidence that had instructed that there be a tiny ducal coronet engraved above the name.

Archduke Niklas, last of his line (indeed, possibly also the first), ushered them into a wondrously vast and decaying room crammed with heavy carved furniture and faded upholstery. The sagging brocade draperies were closed, and only two pale wall sconces gave any light. One corner harbored a yellowing marble bust of a bewigged gentleman, and another was overwhelmed by a massive armoire with tarnished brass fittings.

"May I present Prince Paul Castrocani?" Margaret said. "He kindly consented to drive me when Mr. De Vere could not."

"Castrocani? I believe I know your family. I enjoyed some jolly times with Prince Vincenzo Castrocani years ago."

"My grandfather," Paul said.

"Quite jolly times, they were," the archduke said. He waved a hand at the cluttered room. "I'm afraid I don't have the servants I once did. I keep a little suite of rooms on the floor below." He led them to a staircase that seemed to bring them below street level. "Your grandfather and I, yes. We chased the ladies and gambled a bit together between the wars. He did not care much for that upstart Mussolini, so he stayed away from Italy when he could." The archduke descended the stairs carefully, and Margaret was reminded how very old he must be. "Is your grandfather well?"

"He died some years ago," Paul said. "My father still lives near Rome."

"Vincenzo dead, well, well. Your father would be young Aldo, I should think. I used to see him about the continent some years back with the pretty fair-haired American girl he married. She was very wealthy, I understand."

"My mother," Paul said. "And very wealthy. She has since remarried."

"Ah, well, I hope she saw to his financial needs before

she left him," the archduke said seriously. "That is so very important."

Margaret noticed that in contrast to the dilapidated and dusty condition of the upper floor, the archduke himself was impeccably dressed for his afternoon visitors.

"Here we are," he said, and showed them into a small sitting room that was comparatively dust free and uncluttered. On one wall hung a huge formal portrait of a mustachioed man in a uniform heavy with medals. "Emma fixed these rooms for me," he said sadly. He paused. "She was like a daughter. Rather a granddaughter. I had no children, but Emma was the daughter of a great friend. I knew her as a child, and later we came upon each other by chance. She was alone, as was I. I have been able to give her the benefit of my experience, and she was kind to me. She was beginning to do well for herself."

"But there must be some family, in England perhaps? I assumed she must have been the widow of a titled English gentleman," Margaret said, "to be called Emma, Lady Ross."

The archduke became evasive. "I do not remember precisely how the title came about. But now there is no one." He sounded as though his sadness might well be for his own aloneness. "I cannot even face a memorial service for her."

Margaret said quickly, "You must feel her loss greatly. Is there anything we can do to assist you?"

"No, my dear," the archduke said. "I have become accustomed to losing what I have ever since I was born. We had a good deal when I was a boy, and then the wars came and all was lost." He half raised a finger in the direction of the portrait, as if to indicate that what had been lost was regal and grand indeed.

"Prince Paul and I were wondering, sir," Margaret began, and Paul winced at the mention of his name, "whether Emma might have involved herself in some situation that somehow led to her death."

"Emma was clever and headstrong, but warm and kind. I know of no one who would want to harm her." He paused, and a hint of hidden grief showed in his sad old eyes. "The

policeman who spoke to me indicated a person intent on
robbery had broken in. I cannot believe that it was Marcus
from Navets Nouveaux.''

"He was suspected but released," Margaret said.

"I am relieved.''

"I am curious about the note Emma was said to have left,
saying she would be back,'' Margaret said.

The archduke ducked his old, old head. "I fear someone
has been misled,'' he said. "I did not speak of this to the
police lest they think me a worse old fool than I am, but
Emma left such a note for me a few days ago when I visited
her. She had to go out, and I . . . I must have dozed off. Her
note said that she would return by six o'clock. I left it behind
when I departed before she returned. Did I do wrong in not
speaking of it to the authorities?''

"I should think you ought to mention it,'' Margaret said.
"But the door must have been unlatched,'' she said slowly,
"so guests could simply walk in without ringing.''

The archduke said, "I have a key. I saw the note, but I
had forgotten I had seen it before. It was an old bit of paper.''

Surely Emma would not have left a days-old note lying
about with guests due to arrive. Someone must have found
it among her belongings and left it to be seen by early arrivals
to explain her absence.

"Then,'' said the archduke, "Mr. Dalton arrived with
Miss Corrado and Mr. Wayne, and thereafter a number of
others.''

"So you four were the first, and no one looked for
Emma.''

Suddenly Paul could bear it no longer. "I must go outside,'' he said. "A great honor to meet you, sir.'' He stood
up and bowed to the archduke, then fled to the embrace of
his beloved Ferrari.

"You will have to forgive Prince Paul,'' Margaret said.
"He is in love again.''

"In that respect, not unlike his grandfather and father.''

"Are you certain there was nothing in Emma's . . . business activities that might have led to her death?''

"I did not wholly trust the Dalton fellow, but I have no

reason to think him a murderer. Emma claimed her business with him was insignificant. Some money for her services.''

Margaret did not believe him. "Surely there was more, sir.''

The archduke shook his head. "I did not believe that the other business, about the land, would ever come to anything.''

Margaret leaned forward. "Land? What sort of land?''

The archduke chuckled. "Dry land, my dear, far out in the western part of America. Very little water, no hope of more. No trees, only sand, cactus, and lizards. No oil, no gold, no silver. It was the gift of a dear friend, years ago.'' He looked a bit shamefaced. "I have kept it for the sentiment it represented, but I long ago investigated the possibilities of wealth hidden beneath the sand. There was none. I have the papers about somewhere.'' Then he folded his hands and confessed. "Emma had persuaded Dalton and the Wayne man to buy it. Marie d'Avalon was supposedly assisting Emma in arranging matters. Marie had some idea of creating a beauty spa for wealthy women. She claims to be able to devise substances to make old skin young, unattractive faces beautiful. Slimming diets, painful exercises. Expensive shops to clothe the newly created bodies. Dalton was to invest— perhaps I should say, he claimed to have investors. I did not think much of the plan. To be truthful, I thought it might be dishonest, but I hoped to profit enough from the sale of the land so Emma and I could leave New York.''

"I understand you have a long acquaintance with Marie's family,'' Margaret said.

"I knew her mother well in the old days.'' There was a twinkle in his eye. "Back then we title-rich, cash-poor gents about town had our eyes fixed on rich American girls who wanted to set Paris on its ear. Before the last war, it was. They wanted a jolly good time.''

"And you treated Marie's mother to a jolly good time?''

"Indeed. She was not yet married, but I was not interested in marriage. I had my heritage to consider. She had her fling and went home, and married an American. I heard he was

killed near the end of the war not long after Marie was born—
I was with the Free French.''

"Forgive me for asking," Margaret said, "but could there
be a possibility that Marie is your daughter?"

The archduke shook his head. "None at all. I know that
Marie has said she has claims because of that long-ago romance with her mother, but . . ." He shrugged, as if to
suggest that persons of his status are regularly pursued by the
lower orders. "The family fortune vanished, so she tries any
means to reacquire wealth. For the sake of the past, I try to
be kind to her. It is not easy."

"Would it have been Marie's mother who gifted you with
the worthless land Emma was so eager to sell?"

"Oh yes," the archduke said. "I thought you understood
that. Marie has claimed by rights that it should belong to her,
but there is no doubt that it is mine."

"And in spite of your reservations, Emma's business with
Yale was going smoothly?"

The archduke hesitated. "Last Wednesday when Emma
left the note, she was to meet him. The next day she came
around here with some little things of hers to be stored, and
appeared to be troubled. There were to have been papers for
me to sign, but she indicated that perhaps the time was not
ripe after all. I did not pay much attention, as I was rather
worried that she would be cross with me for forgetting to
carry the bag here the day before. I did not think it dignified
for me to be seen with a shopping bag from Saks Fifth Avenue. She put the bag away somewhere upstairs and rushed
off. I did not see her again."

The archduke was silent, perhaps thinking of the devoted
child who had gone out and never returned.

"This is a very large apartment to care for," Margaret
said to change the subject from Emma.

"It was given to me for my use for life," the archduke
said. "By a dear friend. I could let it out to the students for
a considerable sum, but I was waiting until Emma finished
her business. Then we were going to settle someplace
warm."

The archduke fell silent again, still mourning the loss of

Emma and their plans for the future. Or perhaps . . . Margaret leaned forward and looked at him more closely. The archduke had dozed off.

Margaret didn't hesitate. She wanted to have a look at that Saks shopping bag. This little room was austere except for the archduke's ornate armchair and the grandiose portrait, but upstairs and elsewhere were a hundred places to stuff away a bag of papers. Carefully she edged out of the room. If the archduke awoke to find she had left, he would be too polite to ask where she had gone. She opened several doors off the hallway outside the sitting room. One was the archduke's simple bedroom. The others were either dusty and empty or jammed with old furniture and ancient cartons tied with twine. There was a bathroom with chipped tile, and at the end of the hall a small kitchen with a high window near the ceiling, level with the sidewalk. A kitchen maid could observe the ankles of passersby as she stood at the sink.

Margaret filled a kettle with water and put it on to boil. There was a canister of loose tea and a heavy white teapot on the counter. If the archduke asked, she'd been making him tea.

Margaret opened a door and found the rickety back stairs leading up to the first floor. At the top, she found herself in a narrow hallway that took her to the big room she had first seen. Quickly she looked behind the jumbled chairs and tables, but found no familiar black and red Saks shopping bag. The armoire's shelves were filled with old books, odd bits of geneology, a *Debrett's*, a *Burke's Peerage*, and an *Almanach de Gotha* so ancient that it was probably an historical treasure itself. There was one deep drawer at the bottom of the armoire. It held an array of zippered lingerie cases stuffed with more of Emma's exquisite underwear, bundles of old bills, a case with a few bits of gold jewelry. And hidden under everything, the sought-after Saks shopping bag. It contained more bills, tax returns, letters, a few china objects wrapped in tissue, and a surprise: a slim leather portfolio stamped with gold initials: YAD. Margaret tucked Yale Dalton's portfolio under her arm and sped down the hall, down the back stairs and into the kitchen.

The archduke was still dozing when she set a tray with teapot and cups on a table. Margaret put the portfolio under her handbag, which rested on the floor next to her chair, and said, "Here's our tea, sir. I'm afraid I can't stay much longer. I have another appointment."

The archduke jerked his head upright.

"Tea? How kind. Did I ask . . . ?" He looked a bit befuddled. "I must have dozed off while you were in the kitchen. I do hope you found everything."

"Everything," Margaret said.

Chapter 7

"*You look* guilty," Paul said. He was sitting comfortably in his car surrounded by quadrophonic sound from an invisible source.

"Not at all," Margaret said. She quickly slipped Yale Dalton's purloined portfolio out of sight. "I think it may be too late for us to have tea, if I'm to dress in time."

"Are you seeing De Vere tonight?" He started the engine and listened to it throb. He took a genuine interest in the continuing relationship of Margaret and De Vere.

"Not precisely."

Paul stared up at the leather-covered roof above his head. "I do not understand what that means."

"Absolutely promise not to tell him," Margaret said, "but I am having dinner with a man named Yale Dalton. He was an associate of Emma's. It's a matter of business."

"Naturally," Paul said, "and perhaps a matter of murder as well. Margaret, your habit of detecting has made me suspicious of everything I notice. There is a small window there just at the level of the sidewalk. Would it look in on the lower floor of his Grand Ducal Serenity's palace?"

"It might. Let me think." Margaret closed her eyes and tried to picture the floor's layout. "It would be the kitchen, not the sitting room. Why do you ask?"

Paul shifted gears and eased away from the curb.

"As I sat here, a woman—I happened to notice that she was very beautiful, very desirable, well dressed—came down the street and stopped at the window. She bent down and looked in. Then she stood straight and departed the way she had come."

"When would that have been?"

"Not more than twenty minutes ago. You spent rather more than a half hour with the archduke, you know."

"I might have been in the kitchen then. I made tea." She did not mention her search of the big room. "Do you suppose the archduke has another girlfriend besides poor Emma? Another surrogate granddaughter who is terribly kind?"

"I would put nothing beyond him," Paul said, and expertly propelled the car between two large vans. "I do not think he is what he claims to be."

"Why do you say that?"

"His socks," Paul said enigmatically. They seemed to be moving rather faster than the rest of the traffic, and to distract herself from a possible collision, she tried to puzzle out what it was about the archduke's socks that had troubled Paul. Her late father the earl had occasionally defined a person as a gentleman or not on the basis of some subtle sign that she did not recognize. Something vaguer than the way one sat a horse or treated the servants.

"Socks?" she said finally.

"He wears short socks. An aristocratic person of his age would surely wear high socks with . . . what would you call them? Braces? To hold them up. Such personages do not reveal the flesh of the leg."

"Ah, well. Of course." It was on a par with her noting Emma's poor hemming technique, which was not, as a responsible nanny might say, "a job jobbed."

When they reached Margaret's building, a different doorman was on duty, but he too was instantly smitten by the sight of the car.

"I warn you, my dear Paul, your new mistress is going to be stolen by the next man handy with . . . with whatever is used to start a motor without a key."

"I will hold on to her as long as I can," Paul said. "It

will become expensive to hire or threaten people to guard her.'' He patted the steering wheel affectionately. ''Margaret, you will be careful.''

''There's no danger in a dinner,'' Margaret said.

''In this city,'' Paul said darkly, ''there are dangers everywhere.''

Margaret was frantic to get upstairs and rip open Yale Dalton's portfolio. There was no question that Emma had stolen it, but would it tell her who might have murdered her? Yale was not behaving in an especially guilty manner, but if he had learned that Emma was trying to sell him land on which nothing, not even an expensive health and beauty spa, would grow, might he have been angered? No deal had been consummated, and a man does not normally murder a bit of conniving fluff like Emma out of mere annoyance—unless, of course, Emma had made empty promises that hurt him financially.

The doorman halted her at the elevator and handed her a large square envelope with her name written out in a dramatic italic hand.

''It was delivered when you were out,'' the doorman said, ''by someone in a costume. He looked like . . .'' He shrugged. ''He had a big hat with a feather.''

''Ah,'' Margaret said. She turned over the envelope. A large golden plume had been embossed on the flap. Belinda Hope must have been immediately reminded by Kendall that Margaret had not been officially invited to his party. She opened the invitation as she rode up the elevator. Very nice. She had been invited as a guest of the host, which spared her the necessity of making a contribution to save the species of wildlife endangered by fashion's whim, but more likely to save the giver of the party silly expenses like the food and drink. The party was little more than a week off.

She flung off her coat and opened the portfolio.

There were several interesting items. On top, she found correspondence with Norman Hope from several weeks before, relating to a company that appeared to lease oil drilling equipment. Norman had been offered the opportunity to invest, with the promise of a substantial return on a fairly modest sum. Norman had made the investment and had already seen a profit. Enough, it seemed, to convince him to invest further—and very heavily—with Yale in something referred to as "The Development."

Margaret thought back to Emma's fatal gathering. Belinda Hope had pretended not to know Yale Dalton. Curious.

She scanned the next batch of clipped pages. These were extravagant letters from Kendall Smith, outlining his business plan for a daring fashion venture that would make everyone rich, and presumably, Kenny the richest of all. All it needed was Yale Dalton's backing. A copy of a noncommittal letter from Dalton promised him little. It was difficult to imagine Yale Dalton grasping the implications of a line of haute ready-to-wear clothes for affluent women.

And then Marie intruded, which somehow did not surprise Margaret: a florid scrawl over many pale pink pages, extolling Kendall Smith's genius and her own cleverness.

"You have my assurance," Marie had written, "that the land was the property of my dear, dear late mother, and without question it will revert to me on the death of the old man. Do not believe all that Emma Ross says, my darling, but if you can persuade him to sign now, it will all be as we planned."

What's this? Margaret thought. Although Marie was free with verbal endearments, there seemed some deeper significance in "my darling" writ large in fuchsia ink.

Margaret examined computer printouts that appeared to indicate large sums were involved, but she didn't understand them. De Vere would, but she couldn't ask him. She could ask Paul, but he was bad with figures.

Margaret unfolded a set of blueprints at the bottom of the pile. They appeared to show a large construction project, labeled "Avalon Hills Development." Even if Emma had missed the negative reference to herself, she surely would have noticed the not-too-subtle reference to Marie. She read through the typed pages attached to the blueprints: constructions costs, architect's costs, engineers, tax abatements, financing. It looked authentic. If the plans, as they appeared, laid out an entire city, what a lure for eager investors. But only if it were real and not merely fantasy set upon barren sand.

The very last sheet of paper was an agreement awaiting the signature of Archduke Niklas conveying ownership of hundreds of acres of land to Avalon Hills Development. The sum was a mere twenty-five thousand dollars. No wonder Emma had been troubled. She must have dreamt of much more. And then she had died.

Margaret decided that she would be quite careful of the Dalton gang.

"You sure look pretty tonight," Yale Dalton said. "Blue is just about my favorite color."

Margaret had changed from black to a tailored but feminine brocade jacket and a short blue satin skirt, and very high heels that showed her good legs to advantage. There was no telling where Yale would take her, but she thought she understood what he would like in a woman.

"You're interested in fashion, then?"

"Don't know a thing about it," Dalton said.

He took her to Sal's—more correctly "Sagebrush Sal's," a currently popular restaurant that pretended to be an authentic western café right in the middle of Manhattan, raucous with transplanted (or misplaced) Texans sloshing about with long-necked bottles of beer, which Paul had once informed her were considered convenient out West for grasping as a weapon when bashing an antagonist. Beyond the bar was the dining room done up to look like a frontier brothel (it was described politely in the press as "dance-hall decor"). And beyond that, it was rumored, were good old-fashioned illegal poker games for the initiated.

"How you, hon?" Yale said as Sal herself met them.

"Nice to see y'all," Sal said. She was a sturdy woman who affected a chartreuse gown with a bustle, hair dyed seriously red, and a garnet choker.

"Hell of a gal," Yale said when they were seated in unexpectedly comfortable chairs at a table where the sounds of the country-western jukebox barely intruded. "Started out small in this little town in Oklahoma, made her way East, and look at her now. Sal's amazing.''

"Amazing," Margaret said. She liked the idea that Yale had assiduously reviewed Sal's publicity releases so as to be able to repeat the official story. The true story, as Margaret had heard it from Poppy Dill, was that Sal had begun her career as a restaurateur at a McDonald's near Westport, Connecticut, serving Egg McMuffins and Big Macs to the off-spring of women who wore pastel wraparound skirts and darling little espadrilles. There was a week at an Arizona dude ranch, a stopover at the Dallas–Fort Worth Airport, and the rest was entrepreneurial history.

"Do you know Sal well?" Margaret asked as a frontier hooker waitress placed taco chips and salsa on the table.

"Jes' a bit," Yale said. "We got mutual friends."

Margaret couldn't imagine who Yale Dalton knew in Westport, so she smiled a lot and waited for him to begin discussing the "business matters" that had inspired this meeting. The dining room was filling up: a well-known Greek ship owner arrived with a skimpy female who was quite a bit younger than his youngest daughter; a hugely popular soap opera star with his boyfriend; then a willowy woman with rather odd hair, skin-tight jeans, and long fringe all over her leather jacket. She was with four handsome men. Margaret recognized her as a person mentioned in the press far too often for decency as part of the late-night/early-morning club scene.

The woman caught sight of Yale and swooped down upon him. "We met. Yale, right? At that party at Harriet Fogel's. You were with that woman. She was some kind of royalty."

"I don't quite remember the social occasion in question, ma'am," Yale said, "but I shore do remember you. You must be thinkin' of my dear departed friend Lady Ross."

"I don't think so," the woman said.

"Well, this here's Lady Margaret. . . ."

The woman—Margaret thought she was called something New Age like Astra or Venus or Nebula—looked Margaret over. "Hi," she said, and looked back to Yale. "It was someone with, you know, this serious kind of bosom. Lots

of jewelry. Stunning. Did she come with Kenny? I forget."
She blinked at Margaret. "Did we ever meet before?"

"I doubt it," Margaret said, and took comfort in the sure
knowledge that one day Astra's fleshless body would turn to
total wrinkles.

"Look, we're all getting together later at my loft in SoHo,"
Astra said to Yale. "If you are free . . ."

Margaret did not miss the slight emphasis on *you*.

"Thank you kindly, ma'am," Yale said. "I'll keep that
in mind." He watched her vamp her way to her table.

"I wonder," Margaret said as their waitress sashayed by
and dumped a heap o' ribs on the table between them, "what
business it was that you wanted to discuss with me this evening."

"A little of this, a little of that. I need some help, now
that Emma's not here to guide me."

"I don't know that I could ever take Emma's place," Margaret said sweetly. "What is it precisely that you do, Mr.
Dalton? Mr. Wayne mentioned oil. That being so, I imagine
you must also deal in the land under which the oil exists.
And then on to buildings on the land, and so forth. A veri-
table city." Margaret kept most of her attention innocently
on her ribs, with an eye open for Dalton's reaction.

"You sure do have a good imagination," was what he
said. "Wayne and me do get into oil a bit. Can't seem to
avoid it. But that's not much of a business nowadays. The
real business is leasing the drilling equipment to the guys
who are still dreamin' of oil. These little fellas might have
oil rights or a hunch, but they don't have what it takes to buy
a drilling rig, so they lease it from us. The dreamers do the
huntin' and sweatin', and us practical folks provide the
equipment so's they can dig a big ol' hole at the end of
the rainbow."

"I'm afraid I know nothing of that sort of thing," Margaret said, "but it seems to me that the dear archduke mentioned you were interested in land, specifically some quite
valuable property he owns out in the West. Land is something I do know a bit about. The Priam estates and all . . ."

"The old fella has a bitty parcel someplace," Yale said.

"Poor Emma was hopin' to get me and Wayne to buy it, so's the archduke would have a few dollars to live out his life on. Not my line exactly, but I was tryin' to find a way to do him and Emma a favor. I liked that gal."

"What about the lovely spa for wealthy ladies that Marie d'Avalon keeps mentioning?"

That did stop Dalton for a moment. "Marie? Now there's a real good talker with a heap of imagination. She's always chattering away about this beauty stuff she's concocted, and how all the New York society ladies are just dying to get away someplace nice and have themselves remade. I confess I might of mentioned the possibility, just to quiet her down a bit, and she and Emma got all excited. . . ."

"And Kendall Smith's fashion business."

"I said I don't know a damned think about ladies' clothes," he said somewhat sharply. "That bitty boy is too taken with his own cleverness. Emma was handling him."

Margaret said, "It's too late now for Emma. Who could have done that awful thing to her?"

Yale Dalton shook his head. "Might be we'll never know. What's the old archduke going to do without her? I saw you kindly taking him in hand the other night." He was watching her closely.

Margaret said untruthfully, "He was a very old friend of my father's, so I have taken it upon myself to assist him."

"Is that a fact? Maybe you'll agree to assist me as well."

"Introductions and the like? I might be able to do a bit." She did not want to lose sight of Dalton for the time being, and she had to sound businesslike. How had Emma gone about the delicate task of asking to be paid for services rendered? "About compensation," she began.

"Why, hon, there's no problem there. I'll just see you get the same as Emma did."

Margaret thought for a minute. What Emma "got" was death.

"Perhaps I could help you," Margaret said. "Would you be looking for investors in your projects?" She had a sudden vision of the impeccable Prince Paul posing as an obscenely wealthy young man from Europe eager to invest in a hare-brained American scheme.

"We are allowin' a few select people in on one or two very promising investments," Yale said cautiously.

"Super! Perhaps you could ring me tomorrow afternoon."

"I sure could," Dalton said. He seemed satisfied with Margaret's willingness to work for him. "About the old archduke," he said. "I was thinkin' of paying him a call. Sort of in sympathy. Do you think that would be okay?"

"I don't think he's up to seeing people," Margaret said firmly. "He is terribly distressed by Emma's death."

"It has to do with Emma's business with me," he said. "I ought to retrieve some papers and such she had. I understand she was storin' things at his place."

"I saw no business papers about when I visited him," Margaret said. "But I'd be pleased to enquire when I next see him." She had a picture in her mind of Yale Dalton searching through Emma's apartment for his missing portfolio on the night of her party while Emma's strangled body lay on the bathroom floor. Failing to find it, he was now turning to the next best possibility, the archduke. "My, these ribs are delicious," Margaret said.

"Nothin' like the ones we get back home," Dalton said.

Suddenly the swinging doors to the dining room revealed the massive shape of Wayne D. Wayne.

"Thought I'd find you here, boy," Wayne said. "Evenin', Lady Margaret. You sure look a pretty sight tonight." Wayne D. Wayne had a nervous twitch about one eye and he appeared to be in haste. "I hate to interrupt you folks at dinner, but Yale and me have to talk about some urgent business that's just come up."

Margaret wondered what kind of business came up on a Saturday night. Perhaps one of their investors in a massive metropolis built on the shifting sands was having second thoughts after cocktails at the country club.

"Perhaps I should just say good night," Margaret said quickly, "and catch a cab home. Dinner was lovely, but I know that with you men, business comes first." She hoped the pose of blond idiot woman would satisfy them. It did.

"I can't let you run off alone," Yale said, but he was not eager to dissuade her. "You set down, Wayne, and I'll see that Lady Margaret gets safely on her way." Wayne D. Wayne sank into a chair and mopped his brow. Margaret's last backward glance saw Wayne draining one of those long-necked bottles of beer the waitress had set before him.

As they waited for an uptown cab, Margaret said, "Emma mentioned she'd met you in Geneva."

"I guess that's right," Yale said. "Wayne and I were doin' a little business there, and Tina struck up a conversation with her at a café. It turned out she was right eager to take us in hand. A real pity she's not around to see everything work out. Whoa!" This he called out to a cab which then crossed two lines of traffic to reach the curb. Yale gave her address uptown. His last words were, "Be talkin' to you tomorrow, ma'am."

As soon as the cab pulled away, Margaret redirected it across town to Chelsea. It was a faint hope, but a fervent one, that De Vere would be at home.

She was disappointed to discover that he was not, nor was Paul, but at least she had asked the cab to wait.

"You can take me uptown after all," she said, and sulked a little as the cab plummeted through Saturday evening traffic to take her home.

"Lady M," her doorman said, "your friend is waiting over there. You're a little late."

"Ah, so I am," Margaret said, and grinned at the man who was trying to make himself comfortable on a very uncomfortable lobby sofa. "I've been looking for you, Sam."

"And I for you," De Vere said. "I know that I never seem to go home, but I know that you always do eventually." He took her arm and they walked to the elevators.

"But what about crime in the city?" she said. "You say it never stops. Shouldn't you be out there guarding us civilians?"

"We have better things to talk about than sordid crimes in the city. Don't we?"

She glanced at him out of the corner of her eye as they waited for the elevator. "I known nothing of crime, my dear."

"That's a relief," De Vere said, "although I wonder how long that will last."

Chapter 8

*M*arcus *had* agreed to meet her at ten on Sunday morning. De Vere departed long before that, to return to his pile of computer printouts and incriminating ledgers.

"A mere accountant is what I've become," De Vere had said as he was leaving. "If I had not gone to business school, I wouldn't be where I am today."

"I had no idea you'd gone to business school," Margaret said. "But this is terribly interesting. You can tell me everything about . . ." Then she stopped. She hadn't mentioned a word about Emma or Yale Dalton and Wayne and their business. "About leveraged buyouts?"

"I missed the class on leveraged buyouts," De Vere said. "You look very sexy with your hair messed up that way. I'll call you as soon as I can." He faced her. "Being a cop makes me suspicious, Margaret. You haven't mentioned the Ross murder once, and that is very suspicious."

"You forbade me," she said. "But do you know anything?"

"I am keeping away from that mess," De Vere said. "I understand they took the delivery boy in for questioning, but unfortunately, he probably didn't do it."

"Unfortunately! Whatever do you mean?"

"I mean, unfortunately because now Russo will have to

rub shoulders with people who lie, cheat, steal, commit adultery, indulge in drugs, and commit perjury and murder.''

"I assume you are speaking of my social set," Margaret said.

"You recognize my description," De Vere said good-humoredly.

"They are not all like that."

"True," De Vere said. "Some of them are still infants, and others of them are deceased."

Grand Central Station on a Sunday morning was not throbbing with life. A few passengers stood in line at ticket windows. Derelicts, panhandlers, homeless, and the otherwise distressed had the place pretty much to themselves. Margaret stood beside the information booth in the center of the big domed room and assiduously read the timetables for the Harlem-Hudson rail line.

She looked up at the clock from time to time and saw minutes slip by. Perhaps Marcus had thought better of meeting her. Perhaps he was again in the custody of Detective Russo and his minions.

"You looking for me?" Marcus was much taller than she remembered from their nighttime encounter outside Emma's building. He had broad shoulders and narrow hips, and looked not unlike a very fit track athlete. If Margaret hadn't known that he was in major trouble and was thus unlikely to cause more, she might have found him threatening. As it was, he did unnerve her.

"Yes, lovely. So lovely you could make it." Margaret knew she sounded like an absolute idiot.

"You said you weren't a cop," Marcus said warily.

"Not the police at all," Margaret said. "I was a friend of Lady Ross's."

Marcus said sullenly, "I didn't murder Lady Ross. I told the cops that, and my lawyer made them let me go. I didn't even go into her place except to put down the bags of stuff I brought. On the floor by the door. She gave me a check and I took it back to Pete . . . Pierre at the shop. Man, when he saw it, he was . . ." Marcus struggled to find a polite word for Pierre's French fury. "He was real mad about the check. He sent me back for cash."

"I see," Margaret said, and didn't see at all.

Marcus looked around. He was nervous, too. "This place is full of no-good people," he said. "I rather be out on the streets than stepping over these . . ." He waved a hand at a matted-haired, burlap-wrapped homeless man shuffling through the station.

"Perhaps you'd like a coffee, or something," Margaret said. "Anything."

"There's a deli down a couple blocks," he said. "They got chicken soup with matzo balls this big. Definitely *très supérieur*." He grinned and looked more amiable. He'd picked up a French word or two at Navets Nouveaux.

The soup eaten in silence was very good, but once finished, Margaret faced the prospect of sensitive questions.

"I don't imagine at all that you murdered Emma," Margaret said, "but I have some questions."

Marcus looked at her impassively.

Margaret took a deep breath. "The first question is what time you delivered the food, and why you were hanging about after seven when I left. I suppose you've been asked that."

"Yeah, they asked me. Look, I made her delivery around five. I went back to the shop, and Pierre sends me back for cash. Plus I had another delivery two blocks farther down right off Lexington. I stand around outside her place for a while. I didn't like going back. So I go off to the other place to deliver. The guy is out walking the dog. I wait, so I can get the money, no more trouble from Pierre. The guy could of walked his dog to Navets Nouveaux and picked it up himself, but no. Anyhow, by the time he got back, it's after six. Back to Lady Ross. White folks coming in, going in, all dressed up. Am I going to break in to the party and ask for cash? I hang around some more, and then the cops pull up and I find out she's been murdered."

"What did the police say to your story?"

He looked glum. "The doorman at the building of the guy with the dog, he was temporary. They can't find him yet to say I was there. The guy I delivered to, he's gone too. Took a plane to Jamaica, someplace in the islands.'' Marcus looked as though he wished he were on a plane to any place.

"While you were waiting outside Emma's building, did you notice who was going in? Did you see me, for instance?''

He shook his head. "I was so mad at Pierre, I wasn't looking hard at anything.'' He paused. "But there was something. . . .'' He shrugged. "I don't remember.'' He fidgeted, eager to depart now that he'd told his story. "You said you'd give me something for my trouble. I got to see something before I say anything more. I'm in big trouble, even if the cops did let me go for now. No job, nothing. Ain't going to get a job now, not with the lady dead. I know Pierre's got to think of the customers. They ain't going to want me delivering. And if they don't know, the doormen will. They know everything.''

"This could help.'' She gave him five twenties. "And maybe what you've told me will help you.''

He looked at the money. "It's something. Not what I could make if I were dealing drugs, except my cousin tried that, and he's dead. Fancy car and those rings not doing him any good now. Pierre was teaching me baking.'' He shrugged. "What else do you want to know?''

"When you delivered the food to Emma, the doorman let you in, is that correct?''

"He was in the package room, but he knows me. I yell I'm going up to deliver to Lady Ross, and nobody said anything.''

"How was she dressed?''

"Cops asked me that. I don't know. She wasn't undressed.''

"What was she wearing?''

"I don't know, man. Clothes.'' Marcus looked uncomfortable.

"A dress? Or an old gray robe? Was her hair combed? Did she have makeup on?''

"I don't notice that stuff,'' he said. "I think it was a reddish dress with silver stuff on the front.''

"And she was alone.''

"Yeah. Just her and me, and so I go to jail for a hundred

years. I been delivering to her for months. Same way every time. Put the bag down, take the cash. Sometimes the old guy was there. Nice old guy. He knew how to treat people. 'And how is your mother, Marcus?' 'Dear boy, how good of you to come out in the rain. . . .' You know, he gave me this once.'' Marcus opened his jacket and showed Margaret a round gold medal on a red and gold ribbon. Although Margaret did not know it, it was the Order of the Golden Goblet and Swords First Class—two steps above the order the arch-duke had awarded Marie d'Avalon's one-time husband, the comte.

"Was no one else in the apartment?" Margaret asked.

Marcus got very quiet.

"In the kitchen perhaps, or the bedroom?" she asked.

"I didn't say this to the cops, they'd think I was making up a story to save my ass, but she had this funny smile, not a real smile. And she looked over her shoulder once, like she was listening.''

"Listening?"

"Like she was hoping that whoever was in the other room wasn't going to come out. You think she had a boyfriend with a wife and didn't want him seen? Divorce stuff and all that?"

"You think someone was there then?"

"I ain't going to swear to nothing. If I don't say too much, they got to prove I did it. My lawyer says so. And if I start telling stories about some big Wall Street guy and Lady Ross, they going to cook me good."

"Wall Street?"

"Might have been somebody like that once. 'Oh, Marcus dear, this is my financial advisor, we're going over some papers. . . .' '' He did a fairly good imitation of Emma's fruity English trill. "I ain't no fool, a man tuckin' in his shirt and zippin' more than his lip. But that was before. This time, she didn't look like she'd just hopped out of the sack or was on her way in. She was smiling a fake smile like she was mad inside but she wasn't going to let on to me. I never heard a sound."

"So you wouldn't have any idea if the person was a man or a woman. Think hard."

He closed his eyes. "I'm seeing a table with flowers and candles. Glasses and bottles. Not many chairs. There's a coat or something on one chair. Light colored. That's all. I took the check and left. Pierre never told me not to take her check." He slumped down in his chair and then sat upright. "Hey," he said. "I just remembered. She had something under her arm when she opened the door. Some kind of plastic bag with a zipper. Soft, like she had clothes in it. She put it on the chair with the coat, and got the check and a pen from the table, and filled in the amount. Pierre never told me not to take her check. Now I'm broke and out of work."

"I wish I could help you find another job, Marcus," Margaret said slowly. She was thinking about the bag—a lingerie case, perhaps—under Emma's arm.

"I used to be a bike messenger," he said. "I was good. Fast. Through those cars like lightning, and never hit a body. Only got hit once myself. Mail truck. The government don't teach their people nothin' about traffic laws."

"A messenger," Margaret said. "Of course. Marcus, if I wanted to have a package delivered to a hotel, and not to have known who it came from . . ."

"No problem. You leave it with this guy at the desk. He's the concierge. He signs. No problem."

"Suppose I took it into my head to have someone trailed around the city. . . ."

"If they stay off the FDR Drive, took cabs around the city, you could do it."

"I mean to say, could *you* do it? Tomorrow say? If I found you a bicycle?"

"Nothing illegal," Marcus said firmly. "Nothing the cops could use against me."

"Heavens no, nothing illegal," Margaret said. "We're doing good. We're going to catch a murderer. It's got to be one of these people who are not what they seem, playing with schemes that are less than they seem, if they exist at all."

Marcus looked at her as though she'd taken leave of what-

ever fair-skinned upper-class sense she might have been born
with.

"I am speaking of an interesting challenge," Margaret
said. "And I will pay you . . . thirty dollars an hour."

"I still got my helmet," Marcus said. "It's got this visor,
so no one will recognize me." He was beginning to sound
interested.

"The bike stores must be open today," she said, "to ac-
commodate all these city people who suddenly feel compelled to exercise. And are you free earlyish this evening?
I'd like you to take a look at some people who might be
dangerous."

"That's all you want, lady?" The waiter, having failed by
virtue of his sex at being a Jewish mother, had chosen the
next best thing, being a Jewish deli waiter. He could still get
you to eat and could freely convey disapproval of what you
chose.

"Nothing more, thank you," Margaret said. "Unless
you'd like something more, Marcus."

He shook his head. "I could be around tonight," he said.
"You need a bodyguard? That's a good kind of job. I could
carry a gun."

"I don't need that kind of protection," Margaret said. "At
least not yet."

"I know it's terribly short notice," Margaret said when Yale
Dalton telephoned her on Sunday afternoon, "but I believe
you would meet the sort of people you want to know at a
small gathering I've been invited to this evening."

She had spent an hour with Marcus, purchasing a Fuji
bicycle and a Cobra lock, had reviewed her plan with him,
and had managed to find a place open in Greenwich Village
where she was able to copy all of Dalton's papers from his
portfolio. She had also plucked from the pile of invitations
given her by Poppy Dill the perfect solution to Dalton: a
heavy piece of cardboard elegantly printed with the details
of a cocktail party that evening aboard a rental-by-the-hour
yacht cruising around New York Harbor. It was a corporate
affair, hosted by someone Margaret knew. She thought she

could convince him that it was far better that she, rather than Poppy Dill, was holding the invitation.

"That sounds real good," Yale said.

"There's one more thing, then. I have an acquaintance, quite new to New York. A rather wealthy Italian boy. His father is Prince Aldo Sforza di Castrocani. The Castrocani palazzo is simply magnificent, crammed with treasures. The boy is at loose ends here in America, and I thought you might persuade your Tina to join us this evening and allow Prince Paul to be her escort."

"Our Tina has a mind of her own when it comes to fellas," Yale said.

Margaret said, "The prince might be persuaded to invest some of the family money in your enterprises. Although I couldn't presume to speak for him, I understand the Italians are terribly eager to put their money out of reach of their country's tax collectors."

"I'd be pleased to ask Tina," Dalton said. He sounded as though he had been hooked. "You just stay by your telephone, and I'll call you back in half an hour or so, how'd that be?"

"Perfect," Margaret said. "We're asked for seven, and the yacht sails at seven-fifteen precisely.

"No," Paul said firmly.

"You must," Margaret said. "Come by in your car, hover about in front of the building. We'll hand Tina over to you if she agrees to come, otherwise you'll go about your business. Tina is a very lovely young woman, and besides, there will be lots of pretty heiresses there." Margaret didn't truly regret her fibs.

"I have nothing but bad luck with heiresses. Leila Parkins is engaged to a German automobile tycoon who is three times her age, and Nina Parlons has been named . . ." He could scarcely get the words out. "A vice president of her family's companies. There are no decent heiresses left. All good-looking rich girls are either about to plunge into marriage or are making miserable the lives of filing clerks in large multinational corporations."

"All the more reason to branch out," Margaret said. "Forget about marrying wealth, enjoy yourself. You are far too serious."

"I?" Paul paused to consider. "I believe you may be right in this. The banking business robs one of the joy of living."

Margaret was aware that Paul's duties at United National Bank & Trust were not onerous. The very fact that he appeared fairly regularly at the appointed hour was sufficient to keep his Texas stepfather Benton Hoopes satisfied that he was learning the rules of the straight and narrow life. Paul, however, had not forgotten his carefree days as a Eurotrash youth who preferred Mediterranean sun to institutional lighting, and champagne cocktails to the fare of any executive dining room.

"I will be there," Paul said. "I will be devastatingly charming, if you wish."

Yale Dalton called Margaret back promptly half an hour later. "Tina says she'd be pleased to come. She's getting a mite bored running the business out of a hotel suite. There's just one problem. I hate to leave ol' Wayne D. Wayne here alone."

Margaret had a vision of Wayne D. Wayne pouting at the news that he wasn't to have the chance to cruise around New York Harbor with a tumbler of fine whiskey in his hand and a couple of nubile wenches listening to his tales of the Wild West.

"I know it's not my place to ask," Dalton said.

Margaret was glad he didn't go on to say that Wayne wouldn't take up much room.

"Naturally it would be a pleasure to have Mr. Wayne with us," Margaret said. "I should have thought to ask him."

"What say we swing by your place 'bout six-thirty?"

"Lovely," Margaret said. "We don't want to miss the boat."

"Now I never done that in my life," Yale said. "You take care now."

Chapter 9

*M*argaret *inspected* the limousine that pulled up in front of her building promptly at six-thirty. It was white, it was long, and somehow she was not surprised that it was the very same car that had conveyed Poppy Dill to and from the Zander wedding. The alleged Norman Hope limousine had a more active social life than many an Upper East Side socialite.

"Is there a conspiracy?" Margaret wondered aloud.

"I do not understand," Paul said. He gazed at his beloved, the adored Ferrari, parked at the curb under the watchful eye of a porter from Margaret's building. "But then," he said, "I often do not understand. Ah!" He peered out through the plate glass of Margaret's lobby. "Then there are matters I do not need to understand while liking what I see." A trim ankle emerged from the car. A young woman approached, followed by Yale Dalton. She wore a short full-skirted frock that emphasized curving hips, narrow waist, swelling bosom. Tina Corrado did not appear shy and demure tonight.

"This woman is . . ." Paul stopped. "This is not what I expected, Margaret. Not at all."

Margaret pushed open the door and said over her shoulder, "Try to find out what they're up to in between your passionate sighs. Ah . . . Tina, and Yale. Let me introduce Prince Paul."

Apparently no introductions were necessary. Paul was bowing over Tina's hand, kissing her hand, hustling her toward the Ferrari, ignoring Yale Dalton and Wayne D. Wayne, whose round face peered from the back seat of the limo.

"I'd say the young folks have hit it off," Dalton said.

"Tina looks remarkably . . . seductive," Margaret said, for lack of a better word to describe the kind of emphatic sexiness usually displayed by starlets seeking to make themselves noticed by the people who matter.

"Our Tina likes a good time," Yale said, "but she's a sensible girl at heart. She'll take real good care of your prince."

"I don't doubt that for a minute," Margaret murmured. "Shall we go? What a pleasant car."

"On loan from a friend," Yale said as he helped her in. The driver looked back at Margaret for a second. She met his look with a minutely raised eyebrow. He winked and looked away.

"Well, little lady," Wayne D. Wayne said. "I sure hope you don't think I'm intruding. It gets lonely in the big city for an old fella like me."

Wayne D. drawled on from the East Side to the West and downtown to the pier on the Hudson where the party yacht tied up. This allowed Margaret to ponder in silence whether the plan she had put into action would succeed.

"Never been on a yacht in these parts," Wayne D. Wayne said. "Say, is that boy really a prince?"

"What? Oh, yes. Certainly," Margaret said. "Why else would he call himself that?"

Yale chuckled. "Your friend Lady Ross used to say people could call themselves just about anything they wanted."

"And she was living proof," Wayne said.

"Except that she's not," Margaret said. "Living, I mean to say. I suppose that the police had a great many questions for you, Mr. Wayne, since you knew her so well."

"Can't say I knew her well," Wayne said, and said no more. Margaret had found an effective way to silence Wayne D.

The limo turned into a lot surrounded by a chain link fence

and halted at a building whose empty, cavernous interior was visible past the high open doors.

"Looks like some kind of warehouse," Dalton said. "You sure there's a boat out there?"

"We walk through," Margaret said. She'd passed through similar portals on her way to share in the simple floating pleasures of the immensely rich. "Ah, I see that Prince Paul has managed to find a safe haven for his car."

Paul's car was under guard. A uniformed security guard admired his reflection in the polished lacquer bonnet. And there in the shadows, wearing shades and looking disinterested, was Marcus. Margaret casually took Dalton's arm as though to steady herself. Marcus nodded. He knew the man he was to locate tomorrow. Then several more party goers entered the building. Margaret steered her escorts onto a parallel path as they passed through the building onto the pier, the better to disguise her party-crashing activities. Several mighty yachts were tied up in a row on the long pier, mostly darkened except for dim lights behind portholes where the crews waited for another day and other seagoing galas.

At the very end of the pier, a bustle of well-clad ladies and gentlemen tottered up a gangplank to the deck of a respectably large yacht decked out with festive strings of lights.

"They haven't sailed without us." A shrill woman's voice pierced the dark. "No thanks to you, Norman."

Margaret looked around quickly. Belinda Hope forged ahead with a scowl and Norman in her wake. So intent was she on reaching the yacht, she passed Margaret and her party without a glance.

"The Hopes seem to have been invited," Margaret said.

"It's the sort of thing they like," Dalton said. "Business and pleasure." In the distance, Belinda was well up the gangplank.

The host of the evening, a corporate vice president who had sat with Margaret on several charity committees, was gracious. "Margaret dear, I had no idea you were in town. So good of you to come. So often one's invitations go astray." He looked at her somewhat quizzically.

"Poppy Dill asked me to stand in for her," Margaret said.

"May I introduce Mr. Dalton and Mr. Wayne, who are kindly guiding me through the dangers of New York? Our host is David Curren, a very old and *very* understanding friend."

"A pleasure," the host said. "Poppy has several stand-ins tonight. Prince Paul Castrocani and a lovely young lady are here too. Now, why don't you all find yourselves drinks and enjoy the cruise. I'll find a moment later to catch up with you, Margaret."

"I look forward to that," Margaret said, and she led her band of crashers into the crowd.

The yacht was luxuriously cozy below decks, dark wood, leather chairs, and tasteful chintz, rather more like a men's club than a conqueror of the seas. On the open forward deck were canvas and wicker chairs and a striped awning that left the sides open to the doubtful fresh air of the Hudson River. Attentive youths in white jackets circulated with hors d'oeuvres, and at a mahogany and brass bar the barman poured ample drinks. An up-and-coming young café pianist was coaxing Cole Porter and Rodgers and Hart tunes from an upright piano in the saloon.

Margaret did not see many familiar faces. True, there was a man she recognized as the builder of high-rise condominiums on any available vacant Manhattan lot, and some that were not vacant until he arrived with his bulldozers. There were quite a few sober-suited men who had to be bankers or lawyers, along with expensively but not necessarily fashionably dressed wives. There was a sprinkling of very young and pretty women who were not wives, at least not yet. Norman and Belinda Hope had discovered Dalton and Wayne, while Paul and Tina had found a spot for intimate conversation well forward on the bow.

The host came up behind Margaret and said, "We sail in ten minutes. I had no idea you would be interested in mingling with a bunch of corporate executives, else I would have made it a point actually to invite you."

"I am terribly ashamed," Margaret said, "but I had to take those people someplace. At least they know Norman Hope."

"The Hopes originally sent regrets," the host said, "but

I had a call late this afternoon from Mrs. Hope. She changed their minds.''

"Did she indeed? What's your view of Norman? I know them very little, and nothing at all of his business.''

"In confidence,'' the host said, "I'm beginning to hear rumors that Norman is getting himself in pretty deep in some sort of doubtful schemes in these shaky financial times.''

"Schemes?''

"Would it be shopping centers? Or condominiums? Something that he knows nothing about, to judge from what people say he's been saying. It all goes to prove the old saying that a socially ambitious wife can drive a man to junk bonds. I wonder if he's selling his schemes to your friends.''

"They're not precisely friends,'' Margaret said. "And they are likely to be doing the selling.''

The host looked doubtful. "They won't cause any trouble, will they?''

Margaret tried to look shocked. "Certainly not! Not here. They do seem to be trying to put something over on a nice old man with a bit of money, but I have taken that matter in hand.''

"New York is a wonderful place for exercising our various talents, isn't it? Ah, these must be the very last guests. Good Lord, did I invite them?''

A burst of laughter heralded the arrival of the last party to board. Somehow, Margaret was not surprised to see that it was Kendall Smith and Marie d'Avalon leading a merry pack of revelers. Among them were several women who might be Kenny's models, at the sight of whom a number of the executives tore themselves from weighty chitchat about the state of the stock market and perked up measurably.

"It's Kendall Smith, the dress designer,'' Margaret said. "And party.''

"Ah, yes, he was on the list. One of the corporate wives has taken him up, and asked that he be invited. I suppose she'll get a nice discount for the favor. I do hope they'll behave.''

"Kenny is quite well behaved. His lady friend . . .'' Margaret shrugged. "She's a comtesse. Sort of.''

"Then that's all right. Or is it?" The host had taken a closer look at Marie d'Avalon.

"One can't be sure," Margaret said. Marie was wearing a lavish and wholly inappropriate frock, doubtless the product of Kendall's more feverish imaginings.

The boat creaked and rocked. Some subdued shouts from aft seemed to suggest that the crew was casting off from the pier. Then the engines thrummed and the yacht glided away from its moorings onto the Hudson River.

The host went to see about his guests.

"This your friend's boat?" Dalton joined Margaret.

"Heavens no. This is a company party, some corporation's payoff for past and future favors. My friend is a vice president of something or other, who gets to rent the boat for the night and see that everyone gets tipsy in a dignified way."

"I see," Dalton said. "These fellas look right prosperous to me. Wonder where Wayne's got to? Ah, he's gone up front there with your prince and Tina."

"Forward," Margaret murmured.

"Hell, she's not forward, just a normal young girl. They seem to be hitting it off. Hope Wayne is there to admire the view and not interfere with the young people."

Many of the guests were edging forward to the open deck to watch the island of Manhattan recede as the yacht headed downstream in the direction of the Statue of Liberty. Dusk was falling, and the bright spot of Liberty's torch was becoming visible. Manhattan looked grand from the water. The huge blocks of buildings, old and new, crowding the tip of the island were highly impressive. The senior vice presidents, chief executive officers, chairmen of the board, and the wives who derived their well-nourished lifestyles from the goings-on behind all that concrete and glass were irresistibly drawn to gaze at the splendid scene.

Margaret hung back from the crowd, and presently Kendall was at her side.

"You seem to be following me about," he said.

"I was here hours before you," Margaret said. "New York is rather a small town when you think about it. But I'm curious to know what fascination an event like this holds for you.''

"Please, dear. I'm becoming a titan of commerce." He almost giggled. "These women already buy my couture, and they're going to buy the ready-to-wear. I have a grand plan. Not just the clothes, but Kendall boutiques everywhere. First the flagship shop in New York, close to Armani, I'm hoping. Then London, Paris, Tokyo, Rome, Rio. Then I start to spread like . . . like spilled honey, slowly and inexorably across the United States. To the best malls, the biggest shopping streets. The word 'galleria' will be synonymous with my name. All green marble, and totally luxe. After the ready-to-wear comes the rest. Kendall Smith shower curtains. Kenny: The Fragrance. I don't know about bed linens. Everybody does sheets."

When he stopped for a breath, Margaret asked, "Where do you get the money for all this?"

"One has backers, dear. People know a good thing when they hear it. And I'm a *really* good thing. You did get your invitation to my fête, didn't you?"

"Mmm, I did," Margaret said. "But it must take a lot of money."

"*Everything* takes money," he said. "Tiresome, but true. Marketing will be very, very important to my line. We're going to market *me* as well as my line. People are going to rely on me, on my taste, to guide them. Marie is going to help. She has a very sharp brain."

"Very astute in many matters," Margaret said. "A pity Emma is gone. She might have been a help as well."

"She was useful for a time in making some connections," he said evasively. "And sad as I am that she's dead, she'd rather outlived her usefulness as far as I was concerned." Then he said, "I wonder what will become of the old gentleman. I was thinking I ought to see if there was anything I could do."

"He's being taken care of," Margaret said. "He's not senile or sick, merely old and grieving."

"I had it confidentially from Emma that he's really absolutely loaded."

"He has his assets," Margaret said, "although I am not at liberty to discuss them." Since the archduke suddenly seemed to be everyone's concern, Margaret decided she ought to erect a few barriers until Emma's murderer was found. "I expect I shall be rather involved in his affairs now that Emma is gone."

"I see," Kenny said. "You know, Margaret, you would be perfect to work with me. Your title would—well, simply destroy the competition. I can promise you a really good time, and lots and lots of money."

"At the moment, Kenny, I find I'm quite a bit too much in demand."

"This is such a fabulous idea, I won't let it go," Kenny said.

"I believe you," Margaret said. "Now let's move to the foredeck to enjoy the lights and sights of the city. It's too good to miss."

The yacht was proceeding smoothly past the Statue of Liberty, and the sight seemed to move the guests to patriotic silence.

The sound of the soft tinkling piano drifted out from the nearby empty saloon, and even the busy waiters paused.

Dalton and Wayne and the Hopes pressed against the rail. Kenny was there, Marie and the models, and the corporate chiefs and their wives. Only Paul and Tina appeared unmoved by the view, but when Paul turned on his aristocratic Roman charm, few females were immune.

As the yacht began to leave the statue behind in its frothy wake, some of the corporate gentlemen and ladies opted to replenish their drinks and put thoughts of liberty aside in favor of junk bonds and hostile takeovers.

Then voices were raised on the foredeck. It was impossible to distinguish everyone clearly in the dusk, but Margaret thought she heard Norman Hope's voice, high-pitched and angry, and a rumble of other voices. Wayne D. Wayne's voice boomed out, "Damn fool New York slicker."

"Stop!" An eloquent female screamed, possibly Belinda Hope.

"Look here, now," a man said loudly, and then Marie

d'Avalon's practiced semi-Gallic shriek, which she had been called upon to use frequently of late, pierced the night.

Margaret thought in passing what dreadful manners people had nowadays in public, and Marie shrieked again.

Belinda screamed, "Help!"

The crowd at the rail parted, and where Norman Hope had stood, he stood no longer.

Chapter 10

"*H*onestly," *Kendall* Smith said crossly. "These people simply do not know how to behave. Imagine falling overboard into New York Harbor. Norman will be lucky if there are enough antibiotics in the world to keep him from catching typhoid, tetanus, hepatitis, and hysterical paralysis."

"I can't imagine how it happened," Margaret said, "but I did admire the captain's sangfroid. I suppose he must always be prepared for persons being precipitated into the river."

In the wake of the minor disaster of Norman overboard and rescued handily, the party had come to a quick conclusion. No one, of course, knew anything about how Norman had fallen into the harbor. Once ashore, Dalton and Wayne had put Margaret into Kenny's hands and had taken charge of bustling Norman and Belinda into the white limo for a stop at an emergency room. Paul and Tina had roared away in the Ferrari. Marie had jumped ashore as soon as the gangplank was lowered, and was last seen making her determined way toward Twelfth Avenue and a taxi.

Kenny and Margaret had ended up at a quaint downtown pub for a review of the evening.

"I do blame Marie," Kendall said as he sipped a pale Scotch. "I'm sure she was cozying up to Norman Hope, knowing full well that Belinda can be a witch about things like that.''

"I don't imagine Belinda tossed him over the rail. Or Marie.''

"But Marie's not here to say, is she?'' Kendall feigned a good deal of interest in a cashew he picked from the bowl in front of him. "Ran down the gangplank as soon as we docked. Amazing how fast she managed to move, even in that very tight dress. You know that Emma had a run-in with Belinda, after she found out about her and Norman. After that, they hid their traces much better.''

"It was still going on, then? Norman and Emma?''

Kendall shrugged. "One can't be sure, but I do hope the police are paying attention to that triangle. The Hopes are *very* likely suspects, if you ask me. And there's nothing I'd put past Marie, darling friend though she is.''

Margaret hoped no one wished too hard for a friend like Kendall.

"Emma liked the idea of having a lot of money,'' Kendall said. "She could be very greedy.''

"Perhaps,'' Margaret said, "but for all her faults, I loathe the idea of her being strangled in her own home, dressed to kill, as it were. . . .''

"That's a bit of an exaggeration,'' Kendall said. "She wasn't actually wearing my dress, or was she?'' Kendall peered anxiously at Margaret through his round glasses. The candle on the table reflected back from the lenses. "How utterly ghastly.''

"No, she wasn't,'' Margaret said. "She was in her robe.''

"The building super was very taken with her. I've seen Harry eyeing her many a time. Not that I think for a minute Emma would encourage him, but people have been known to do the strangest things when they're behind with the rent.''

"I don't believe it of Emma. I would say she would have been spurred on to find the rent. Do I understand that you were often at her place?''

"Not really. The salon is quite close by.''

"What I mean is, didn't the place look to you as though she was on the brink of clearing out?''

"She was," Kendall said. "Take the money and run."

"But *what* money?" Margaret asked.

"She was going to do all right if she'd continued to do a few things for me. Not a lot, you understand, not what I have in mind for you."

"No business, Kenny," Margaret said. "Not tonight."

"Oh, dearest ladyship, *please* take a look at my business plan. It's too wonderful. At least think about it. And maybe we can even do something for the old archduke."

"I think not," Margaret said, quite definitely.

"Lordy, look at the time," Kendall said suddenly, and stood up. "I ought to take you to dinner, darling, but I have to meet some people. Do you mind? Can I drop you someplace?"

"Run along," she said, and he made a kissing face in her direction and dropped some bills on the table.

"By the way," he said, "I was standing fairly close to Norman when it happened, and I could swear that I heard that thug Wayne D. Wayne threatening him. 'You know what happens to people who double-cross us'—that sort of thing. The man is frightening. So long, milady." Then Kenny was gone.

When Margaret emerged alone, Kenny had disappeared.

She wondered all the way home about the frail and saddened old archduke in his dusty apartment thinking about lively Emma, Lady Ross, who would not again be there to pretend and please, serve and listen. She wondered if there really were piles of bankbooks, yellowed stock certificates, and ancient jewels hidden away in the apartment's nooks and crannies that needed looking after.

Impossible. The product of Emma's fantasies.

"I ought to look in on him," Margaret thought.

"I cannot *believe* your behavior. I was absolutely *humiliated* in front of all those women, people I wouldn't ordinarily even *speak* to. It's going to be all over town, and I won't be able to lunch anywhere without knowing that every eye in the room is on me."

Norman Hope closed his eyes and allowed his wife to rant

without interruption. Blankets were tucked around him, and his body throbbed: a nasty bruise on his thigh where he had been bounced off the rail against a vicious brass bolt. His buttocks had been punctured by syringes pouring anti-this and anti-that into his river-soaked body, his lungs were sore from gasping for breath in the chilly water, and his arms ached from flailing about at the foot of the Statue of Liberty.

At least, he was thinking sleepily, he understood that there had been great progress in cleaning up the Hudson's pollution—although he didn't imagine that the harbor had yet returned to the pristine state when—was it the Dutch? the English?—had first recognized that Manhattan Island was ripe for real estate development.

"I wish you would explain clearly and simply, in words of one syllable or less, exactly what happened." Belinda was not through with him yet. "I can't imagine what Yale and Wayne are thinking now."

Norman thought of one-syllable words behind his closed eyes. *Argument* had three syllables. *Dispute* had two. *Money* likewise. *Sex* was all right syllabically.

"Mad," he mumbled finally.

Even that one-syllable effort failed to please Belinda. "I'll say. You're totally mad. A stupid fight on a hired yacht in front of some of the most influential businesspeople in the city. What will everyone think?"

Norman struggled half-upright on an elbow and said, "Maybe they'll think it was an unfortunate accident, and will express their sympathy. Anyhow, it's nobody's business but mine."

"Ours," Belinda said coldly, and turned on her heel. She slammed the door of her own large bedroom across the hall in the Hopes' large and far too expensive apartment. At least the children—those three young hopes of the Hopes—were away at school. Belinda's theory was that if the two girls and the boy, all of them approaching teen-age, were out of sight, she would not be viewed as old enough to have nearly grown-up offspring. The private school fees were burdensome, but one had to make some sacrifices as a parent.

"Damn Emma Ross," Belinda said aloud to the art deco

mirror that reflected an art deco room that was already passé. Almost time to redecorate. "Even in death . . ."

An hour or so later, Marie d'Avalon was safely installed at a corner table in an impersonal lounge in an impersonal hotel where no one she knew would possibly come.

Finally someone she did know arrived about the time her patience had evaporated. She signaled angrily.

"I have been waiting for hourrrs. I do not have hourrrrs to waste." Then she shrugged, a gesture copied after long hourrrs of observing the French shrug and polishing her act. "No matter. You're here, and now we will talk. What a drrrreadful evening. What possessed Wayne to push Norman into the sea in front of all those people? Stop fidgeting and sit down. What have you to tell me?"

The conversation seemed to interest Marie. "We will have to be careful," she said. "I wonder if this wretched Lady Margaret is going to cause problems. I have heard that she puts her nose into everything, especially murders."

Very much later that night, Archduke Niklas sat in a throne-like armchair in his decaying palace on Riverside Drive. Earlier he had received a message delivered to his door from Yale Dalton, begging for an opportunity to pay a call, and he had spent some hours pondering what he should do. He did not trust the man, not at all. He had spent too many decades sizing people up and had survived by being right about them most of the time.

From time to time, he moved about his sitting room to touch a few of the little treasures that represented a real or imagined heritage. Without Emma, they had lost some of their shine.

Into whose hands would they fall when he was gone? he wondered. He had thought that Emma might have them one day. She would come back here after a dignified and quiet memorial service to mark his passing, and open the box where he kept his medals and orders, his papers, the handful of letters from very very famous and titled personages, the ring that had been worn by the last king. Emma would shed a few tears, recalling the evenings they had spent while he talked of the old days. She had listened, although she had not really understood the history of armies that marched and ravaged peasant villages, leaving behind mangled bodies and burning cottages. She heard the tales of romances and marriages that joined titles and lands, of kings reigning and deposed, and of their kingdoms that had fallen apart three quarters of a century ago. She would retain his tales and his treasures when he was gone.

Then the archduke shook his head. He had forgotten. It was not he who was dead, but Emma. So hard to believe. He could almost imagine he heard her footsteps on the floor above, as she rummaged about in the old chests and opened boxes to examine the fascinating bits and pieces of his old life. What a life it had been. . . .

The archduke nodded and fell into an old man's sleep.

The footsteps above did not rest.

Chapter 11

Detective Russo was brief and businesslike, early on a Monday morning.

"De Vere swears you couldn't be the murderer," he said. "I got to believe him. You weren't the murderer the last time we met, either."

"Mr. Russo, I can assure you that I had it so ingrained in me by my late mother that murder is basically wrong that it would take the severest provocation even to contemplate it. Emma Ross had no reason to provoke me in recent months." Margaret regretted her flippancy at the sight of Russo's face.

He leafed through a sheaf of papers. "Nobody who was there that night knows a thing. Everyone's whereabouts before they arrived are so far proven. Now tell me again about this party."

Margaret told him. She was factual, just as she'd promised De Vere: Dalton at the door, the arrival of the Hopes, of Kendall Smith, the discovery of Emma's body by Marie, the arrival of the police. She took a deep breath and explained about the misleading note and the archduke's faulty memory. "I'm sure he's telling the truth," Margaret said. "He's harmless, and he was very fond of Emma."

"Yeah, and he seems to have had a prowler last night. He told a neighbor, who told the police. They got bad security in that building, and the old guy apparently is lax about locking up. The report got sent over here from the West Side because of the murder.''

"It would be a kindness if the police could watch out for him," Margaret said. This new development worried her.

Russo said, "Lady, do you have any idea what kind of stuff we got goin' down in this city? We got so much trouble, we have to see blood or a lot of bullet holes before we get men and time to watch out for some old guy who forgets to lock his door.''

"I do understand," Margaret said, genuinely meaning it. She had thought of a plan and was eager to get on with the interview.

"Okay," Russo said. "The murder couldn't have been done while you were there." He was stating a fact.

"No.''

"She could have been murdered by the first guest, except that was the old archduke. So it was before." Russo rubbed his forehead. "The kid did it," he said. "I shouldn't be saying that to you, but I feel it in my gut. We're still looking at the super, but he's got an alibi.''

"The kid?" Margaret asked cautiously.

"The black kid, the delivery boy. De Vere spotted him outside when you were leaving. He brought over some kind of fancy take-out food for the party around five. We figure this buxom dame in her robe opens the door, he thinks he can pick up some jewelry, some cash, so he kills her, probably by mistake. I don't think he found a thing. The place was practically bare.''

"Emma was in the process of moving, I believe," Margaret said. "Are you certain it was the delivery boy? Did he tell you she was wearing a robe?''

Russo grimaced. "He said a dress, but he could have seen it hanging up in the john when he strangled her. We didn't have anything to hold him, and anyhow, his mother sent a lawyer. We're keeping an eye on him. He says he didn't do it.''

"Wouldn't you, particularly if you had not?" Margaret stood up. "If you're finished with me . . .''

"Not quite," Russo said. He lifted a sheet of paper, and

Margaret sat down. "I picked up pretty quick from people who were there that this Lady Ross has been fooling around with . . . ." He consulted the paper. "Mr. Norman Hope of Park Avenue. You know anything about that?"

"Only the rumor," she said. "You know how people talk, especially when sex is involved. I don't know the Hopes well, and as I said, I haven't seen much of Emma in the last year or two. She never confided in me."

"I thought you Brits stuck together. Lady This and Lady That."

"I should tell you, Mr. Russo," Margaret said, "that Emma Ross truly . . . might not have been what she seemed, what she called herself."

Russo shrugged. "Who is? I'm not really a policeman. I'm really an all-star shortstop. Hey, what can I say? In my head, that's who I am. What about the archduke fellow? Is he who he says he is?"

"Like you, in his head he's really someone other than he seems," Margaret said. Russo looked blank. "I mean, he's not really a frail old man living in reduced circumstances. He's really the rightful ruler of whatever country he came from. In his head."

There was a gleam of understanding. "Gotcha," Russo said. "There's one more thing. The other people there, this Yale Dalton, Wayne Wayne . . . ."

"Wayne *D.* Wayne," Margaret said.

"Right. That countess who fainted, a Mr. Smith, a bunch of other people. None of them know anything."

"They wouldn't, and I can't say that I know anything much of them. Mr. Dalton and Mr. Wayne are out-of-town businessmen. Mr. Smith designs expensive dresses. The comtesse has designs."

"I didn't think you'd know anything. Thanks for your help."

"Why, I've been no help at all," Margaret said, "except that I was almost the first to see Emma's body. I'm sure you noted that she was just lying there, strangled and ugly. But no disarray. Nor struggle, it would seem. No evidence of a drug-crazed youth seeking valuables. I don't know much about these things, but it seems to me that a youth intent on robbery and murder might have been more . . . disorderly.''

''There's something to that,'' Russo said. ''We were wondering if maybe she invited him in? For . . . you know.''

Margaret responded to his suggestion with a look of disdain. Emma Ross might have used sex and charm and a title to enhance her status, but Margaret did not believe that she would have been overcome by a sudden desire for a young delivery boy whom she had apparently known for some time.

''I didn't think so,'' Russo said. ''We'll keep an eye on him just the same.'' He sounded as though the murder of Emma, Lady Ross might be relegated to the Interesting But Not Urgent list.

Margaret said, ''I don't care for the idea of an acquaintance of mine being murdered, and no one to answer for it.''

Russo looked tired, and it was only a bit past ten. ''Believe me, Lady Margaret, I don't like the idea myself. But I think you might be talking about a kinder, gentler city where the thousand points of light are candles under the chafing dish and on some kid's designer birthday cake, rather than those in abandoned buildings where the homeless hang out or the ones mothers on welfare use for light when they can't pay Con Edison. We'll be in touch.''

He dismissed her by returning to the papers on his desk.

''De Vere's still downtown,'' he said without looking up.

Margaret merely nodded. De Vere had told her that he would be out of touch for most of the week as he sifted through incriminating computer printouts. Margaret had remarked that she didn't care much for a society where microchips devised on the other side of the Pacific Ocean could incriminate a hardworking criminal.

She left the precinct building, wondering how everybody's preferred suspect, Marcus, was doing.

Marcus was doing well, even though he was not yet entirely certain what he was doing. At least he knew who to look for.

Margaret's first instruction was to be at the Hotel Villa d'Este at eight in the morning in the guise of a bicycle messenger. He was to put a leather portfolio into the hands of the concierge, to be conveyed anonymously, with due ceremony, to Mr. Yale Dalton, honored guest of the hotel.

"It was . . . borrowed without permission and must be returned quietly," Margaret had explained to Marcus, in the belief that one's employees should know something of what was happening and why. "While it is out of his hands, he is uneasy because his secrets are loose in the world."

Marcus shook his head. "When he gets it back, he still going to know that somebody probably looked at his stuff, 'cause somebody sent it back to him. What if he figures the somebody was you?"

"What you say makes a good deal of sense, Marcus," she said. "I will take precautions."

The delivery part was easy, although Marcus was conscious that his presence in the luxuriously appointed lobby was not entirely pleasing to hotel personnel. The concierge hastened to receive the portfolio, sign an authentic-looking delivery receipt Margaret had devised, and point him toward the exit.

When Yale Dalton emerged from the hotel at nine, Marcus at his watching post in a public telephone kiosk across the street saw that the portfolio or one like it was tucked under his arm. Mission accomplished. Dalton got into a long white limousine. Marcus was relieved that he wasn't to be following an ordinary yellow cab. He put on his helmet, lowered the visor, and maneuvered the new bike into traffic as the white car pulled away from the hotel entrance.

Since he was not being paid to make judgments, merely to note locations, it did not matter much to him that Dalton was driven a comparatively short distance to a Park Avenue apartment building with an awning, a doorman, and a four-digit number. Dalton got out, walked to another awning two doors away, and waited, while the limo remained in front of the apartment building. A few minutes later, a man rushed out, briefcase in hand, and threw himself into the back seat of the limo. The car moved away, and as soon as it hit the first downtown light, it turned left and headed east. With the left turn accomplished, Dalton strolled back to the original building and disappeared inside.

Although still unjudgmental, Marcus was becoming curious. He was sure the recently departed second man was someone he had seen the night before at the pier, when on Margaret's instructions he was taking note of Yale Dalton.

There weren't many places for a young black man with a bicycle to loiter on Park Avenue. In fact, he had already spent too long pretending to examine his pad of delivery receipts by the time the limo departed.

Then he noticed a service truck pulling in front of a gray stone building across the avenue. The repairman was an older man who might be made an ally. The repairman went around to the back of his truck and took out a snaky length of piping and a tool box. Marcus didn't hesitate. He whipped along the cross street on his bicycle, defying traffic lights and the traffic in the time-honored tradition of New York bike messengers.

"Hey, man, I'm waitin' for this dude," Marcus said. "I work for this private detective, see, and . . ."

"I lock up this truck real good when I leave her," the man said. "I have alarms. No way you goin' to get inside."

Marcus spread his arms wide in utter innocence. "Not me, man. I just need a place to watch, outta sight. Ain't no drugs or robbery or anything like that going down."

"You want to sit in my shade, you sit. Be my guest. But I'm right there in the front window. I got a place to watch you." He started to walk away, then turned back. "You tell anybody who asks that you are working with José, who is fixing the ventilation in Dr. Berinstein's office."

"Right. Thanks." Marcus settled down to observe the apartment building across the avenue.

More than an hour passed before Yale Dalton reappeared. Marcus was poised to follow, but this lap was tougher. Dalton walked west from Park toward Madison with Marcus backpedaling so as not to overtake him. On Madison, the quarry entered a narrow doorway. One floor above street level, Marcus saw the broad expanse of window with posed figures dressed in gowns that seemed to be made entirely of feathers. He saw movement beyond the mannequins in the window, and then nothing. Twenty minutes later, Dalton emerged from the doorway and flagged a passing cab. This was going to be harder yet. The cab turned right, back toward Park, and on Park headed downtown.

Marcus met the challenge. The cab turned left at the Helmsley Building at Forty-sixth, reached Second Avenue, and zigzagged through traffic to the East Thirties. About the time Marcus thought he might not manage to keep the right cab in sight, it stopped near a massive red brick apartment building. This was more of a neighborhood than Park Avenue—shops and delis and even some benches under city-planted trees where a hardworking messenger could take a break and nobody cared. But he kept his eye on the red building Dalton had entered, and fifteen minutes later was rewarded by the arrival of yet another person he had seen the night before. This one was the woman who had been in the company of the guy with the incredible Ferrari.

And half an hour after that, the same white limo rolled up and Dalton and the woman came out with a second woman who looked to be some kind of hooker, to judge by her clothes. (Marcus was clearly not attuned to Marie d'Avalon's tastes.)

Marcus shook his head. These people. It was like watching some kind of movie. He attempted to follow the limo, but to his regret, it was on its way to the FDR Drive. He gave up and called Lady Margaret from a pay phone.

"Not to worry," she said. "I have a fair idea where they might be headed. Perhaps you should go back to the hotel and wait to see when Dalton gets back. Could you manage that?"

Marcus was doubtful. "People are going to notice me hanging around," he said.

"Do the best you can," Margaret said, "and then come round late this afternoon to report everything in detail."

Fortunately, he did not have to pose as a conspicuous idler for long. First the tall, dark young guy with the Ferrari arrived at the Villa d'Este, and hung about the front entrance until Dalton and the young woman returned shortly thereafter. Marcus pedaled the bike uptown to tell his tale to Lady Margaret.

* * *

"Such a peculiar story you're telling me," Margaret said. "But I believe we'll keep you out of prison yet. Dalton to Belinda to Kenny to Marie to Norman. Fascinating."

Marcus was glum. "If anybody had caught on today . . ."

"Nonsense. You're far too clever to be caught, and besides, you were doing perfectly innocent things."

"Lady, I'm always doing innocent things, and it don't make much difference. I carry some bags to Lady Ross, doing my job, and they trying to pin a murder on me."

"It will be all right," she said. "Trust me. Let's see, Dalton saw everybody. . . ."

"Don't forget that prince with the car."

"He was acting upon my instructions. Not willingly, but he's a good boy. While all this is going on, Wayne D. Wayne was paying a call on the archduke."

"I don't know about that," Marcus said.

"I do," Margaret said. "I got to the archduke first, and we didn't answer the bell, but I saw him."

"Do you have a guest?" A faint, slightly accented voice came floating down the hall. "I do not mean to disturb you, dear Lady Margaret. . . ."

Archduke Niklas came hesitantly into the room and brightened at the sight of Marcus. "Marcus, my boy. How good to see you. Are you well?"

"Yes, sir." Marcus stood up.

"The archduke was feeling very much alone," Margaret said, "so I invited him to stay, since I have the extra room. Security at his building is not what it should be."

"Just a day or two," the archduke said.

"Until things are clearer," Margaret said. "There's still much to be done."

"You want me tomorrow?" Marcus asked. "I kinda like this detective stuff."

"I imagine I might," Margaret said. "Could you ring me this evening? You can leave the bicycle here. I'll give you cab fare home."

Marcus was able to laugh for the first time in a while.

"Lady, ain't no cab driver in this city goin' to take this black boy to Brooklyn, even if I show him a hundred bills."

"Aren't they required . . . ?"

Marcus shook his head. "Don't you worry. I know my way around the subways."

After Marcus had left, Margaret settled the archduke in front of the television set to watch Donahue interview a group of persons who might have been men in drag, and telephoned the Villa d'Este.

"Tina dear," she said. "It's Lady Margaret. We do need to talk. I'm still at a total loss about what I can do for Yale. He's such a . . . such a dynamic personality. So charming, so *worthwhile*. We talked the other evening, of course, but I do need guidance that only you can give. One or two little problems have popped up. No, no, nothing serious. Could we lunch tomorrow?" She paused to listen. "I don't often do breakfast," she said, "but I do understand it *is* the thing nowadays. The Trevi Room at the Villa d'Este at eight, then."

Margaret was pleased by the day's work, even though unsure of what it all portended, and definitely doubtful about a power breakfast with Tina at such an early hour. She was not at her sharpest at eight in the morning, unless it was with the prospect of riding a good horse through the woods back home in England at Priam's Priory.

"I will be brave," she said aloud to herself, and dialed Paul's business number. "And I will be fully awake."

Chapter 12

*M*argaret reached Paul just as he was leaving his desk at United National. "Since you saw Tina today and the others," she said, "you are obliged to report what you discussed."

"Business," Paul said. "Margaret, you cannot imagine how much money I will earn from a very reasonable investment."

"My dear, you have nothing to invest."

"My mother . . ."

". . . is too wise to put her money in a scheme that appears to be built upon sand," Margaret said. "Did Dalton and Wayne discuss a development called Avalon Hills?"

"They suggested that details of such a project should be considered highly confidential. I do not understand why they should name a large undertaking for Marie d'Avalon, but it appears to be the case. She is to have a health spa which will attract the rich and famous. However, they did not exert exceptional pressure on me to invest."

"Perhaps they are being cautious, what with Emma's murder still hanging over them, and that particular channel to the archduke closed. What do you make of Tina?"

There was a longish pause. Then, being a fairly honest young man, he confessed. "I didn't tell you last evening," he said, "but it was Tina I saw looking in at the archduke's windows the other day while you were visiting him. I suppose I should have spoken at once, but I did not wish to hinder my pursuit of the lady.''

"Oh dear," Margaret said. She was startled indeed by the news. "You said nothing to Tina, I trust."

"Naturally not," Paul said. "I am posing as a stranger in New York, and know you only in passing. And she did not notice me that day. She is not one, it seems, to pay heed to autos, even ones as beautiful as mine."

"So that trio must have known all along that I was with the archduke the day after Emma's murder. No wonder Yale was so eager to acquire my services."

Paul said, "As it happens, Mr. Wayne mentioned some concern about the archduke to Dalton. It seems there are matters pending that they did not explain to me."

"I should not like to see the old gentleman in peril. I know, you remind me he is likely not quite a gentleman, but still, he is old and kind."

"Peril?"

"Possibly someone got into his apartment last night. No harm done, nothing taken, but there is a murderer about." She decided to keep secret from Paul her earlier extraction of the portfolio from the premises and its subsequent return to Dalton.

"They spoke of the archduke," Paul said, "perhaps to impress me with their connections. They conveyed that he is an important partner in their enterprise. They explained that my prospects for acquiring wealth from an investment were related to the land that the archduke possesses. Is any of this possible?''

"Not precisely," Margaret said, "although I do believe the archduke continues to be of value to them for the present. Did they give you papers—blueprints or a prospectus?"

"I have some things," Paul said. "I thought you might wish to see them. Expensively produced brochures. The information given is most convincing."

"I will send a messenger to fetch them from you at the bank in the morning," Margaret said. "I am breakfasting with Tina tomorrow. Early meetings are an aspect of this city that I have not yet assimilated into my lifestyle.''

"And I," Paul said, "am taking Tina to dine this evening." He hesitated. "Is it right that I should continue to be attracted to her when she might have been party to a murder? And is it right that I am acting as something of a spy, all the while finding her attractive? Matters were never so complicated when I pursued girls on the ski slopes and beaches."

"I understand that Lucrezia Borgia had a multitude of admirers, in spite of an unfavorable reputation."

"She has been greatly maligned," Paul said, "and I say that even though I cannot count her among my ancestors." He sighed. "I will tell you if Tina says anything of interest regarding investments or murder."

"What, may I ask, do you two actually talk about?"

"Cities, resorts, airlines we prefer. She has traveled widely, as Dalton's business takes him everywhere around the world. She does not like Moscow, she enjoys Hong Kong for the shopping. Then I tell her she is beautiful, desirable, charming, and she extolls the pleasures of Ibiza and New Orleans."

Margaret was thoughtful as she regarded the archduke leafing through a copy of *Tatler*, pausing now and then to examine the candid photos of the British upper classes at play. Dalton was less and less an innocent country boy and more and more a worldly manipulator. She hoped sincerely that he didn't truly believe that the archduke was secretly wealthy, or that by disposing of him his land would become Marie's to give away to him.

To deflect the hounds from the archducal quarry, she truly would have to take Emma's place convincingly. It must be made known that she was not merely assisting the archduke, but that she had been given the power of yes or no over all decisions relating to him.

"Would you care to go out to dine, sir?" Margaret asked.

"Oh no, my dear. I seldom go out these days." The archduke sounded somewhat wistful.

"I know of a quiet place with excellent food," Margaret said. "You might enjoy it."

Archduke Niklas made a gracious, graceful gesture with his long, pale hand. "I always enjoy the company of a beautiful women," he said.

"Then we shall go. It's just around the corner, and none of that *nouvelle cuisine* nonsense. Good cream in the sauces, good butter for the bread."

"Ought I to wear my cape? Emma says that people here don't always understand the cape, but I find it comfortable. I have worn one for years."

"You should wear what pleases you," Margaret said. "And never be a slave to fashion."

The archduke smiled faintly. "Never fear. Yet fashion was much on the mind of poor Emma," he said. "That Smith fellow she thought so highly of—I did not understand why she believed he had the touch of the great ones. I remember women dressed by Dior, and that Spaniard, Balenciaga. Madame Chanel and I were a bit more than nodding acquaintances, you know, in the old days. And Elsa Schiaparelli—there was a clever woman." There was a gleam in Archduke Niklas's eye as he seemed to view again the beauties of the past. "What is being done these days to the woman in the name of fashion . . ." He shook his head. "Years ago, women were made to look feminine, beautiful."

"What do you think of Kendall Smith's work?" Margaret said, as the archduke donned his cape.

"He had taken Emma up rather actively," he said. "For a time, they were as close as can be. I did not think him suitable for various reasons. He is, after all, in trade. Marie d'Avalon was forever praising his couture, but I thought he made the ladies look rather like *poules de luxe*. I thought him shallow, with more talk than talent. Well, what does an old man know?"

Margaret thought perhaps this old man was more knowing than he let on.

The restaurant had been discovered by the right sort of people: those who liked a small, comfortable place, excellent food and service directed by the pleasant young man who owned it and did the cooking. Margaret understood that he had threatened a lawsuit if any reviewer dared to mention its name in print. Once a few stars were placed beside a New York restaurant's name, the patrons of fashion, rather than of food, descended in hordes and reshaped the place to their own vision.

The waiter knew immediately to make exactly the right amount of fuss over them. It might have been because Margaret and De Vere were frequent patrons, but more likely because the archduke carried an aura of dignity and importance, whoever he might have been at the beginning of his adventure. Living proof, perhaps, that wishing will, indeed, make it so.

The archduke dropped his cape into the waiter's waiting arms and nodded with satisfaction at the heavy silverware, the good wine glasses, and the thick linen napkins. The owner appeared from the kitchen.

"If your excellency will entrust me with dinner?"

"I advise you to do so," Margaret said.

"Wisely said, Lady Margaret," the owner continued. "I've been holding back some perfect veal for the right persons."

The archduke beamed, and Margaret hoped he would not extract a decoration signifying honorable service to the archducal stomach. Happily, he did not, although he might feel compelled to do so at the end of the meal.

Archduke Niklas shook a playful finger at Margaret. "Do not allow me to overindulge in food and drink. I am no longer either accustomed or fit enough to do so. Emma was good about looking after me." The moment of sadness passed quickly.

"I confess I simply do not understand what she was up to," Margaret said. "Or why she had to die."

He looked at her for quite a long minute. "You would like to know why, so as to know who." The archduke took a careful sip of the wine the waiter poured and nodded. His glass was filled, and Margaret's. "I do not know," he said. "She is gone, so what I say now cannot betray confidences."

"I should think that confidences are overruled by murder," Margaret said. "And I have been making a few enquiries about her associates." She waited while he thought.

"Emma was not what she pretended to be, but surely you were aware of that. She was born in England. Her mother was a woman of excellent qualities, but sadly alone. Dora confessed once that she was never able to master the typing machine, and the telephone confused her. She did not succeed as a shop girl, but men found her extraordinarily attractive, so she turned to the only means she knew to make . . . substantial sums. Do you understand me?"

"I understand that she was perhaps . . ." Margaret paused to find the delicate word. "A sort of courtesan?"

"Exactly," the archduke said. "We met at a fête of some sort when I was visiting London. She accompanied a very highly placed personage. Very high. I saw a bit of her, but not, shall we say, professionally. She was merely a young woman in need of a friend. This was perhaps twenty-five years ago. Emma was a lovely child of five or six who used to sit upon my knee. The little daughter I never had."

The waiter brought fruit and cheese. The archduke nibbled grapes and continued to look back into the past Emma had risen from.

"There was some scandal," he said, "involving Dora and one of her highly placed personages. Hard times came for her, and she emigrated to Australia. I helped with the passage. Emma wrote to her Uncle Nicky over the years, and Dora's last letter before she died—quite young, alas—asked that I do what I could for Emma if the occasion arose. I learned by chance that when she was grown, Emma came home to England and lived there for some years. We met again at last here in New York." The archduke looked at Margaret and shook his head. "Emma herself never mastered the typewriter. In this and other ways, she took after her mother. But Emma was somewhat more ambitious."

"Emma, you know, pretended to a background and family similar to mine," Margaret said. "It was a fantasy, but we both joined in the pretense."

The archduke nodded. "I understood that. She found her title in the deaths column of the London *Times*, I believe. No harm done. She was not of our class, but I do miss her. . . ."

"Do you have any suspicions of who might have murdered Emma? It was certainly not Marcus, the young man from Navets Nouveaux."

The archduke dismissed the idea of Marcus. "I have no suspicions. Emma had what we used to call a 'past,' but it was not sordid, simply foolish. I do not believe a person from her earlier adventures reappeared to strike her down." He pondered. "Could it have been a jealous woman? Emma was most attractive to men, and these people . . ." He waved his hand. ". . . this Dalton and Wayne seemed quite interested in her. She claimed it was entirely business. I warned her against trusting them too much. I have been in this world far longer than she, and I can see past the facade. I even warned her that men like Dalton and Norman Hope very often have wives or women in the background who do not take kindly to another woman."

"Such as Marie d'Avalon? I have heard rumors." Margaret spoke carefully.

"I do not approve of Marie," the archduke said sternly. "But I would not yet accuse her of murder. I would think sooner of this girl Tina Corrado."

"Tina? Why so?"

"She has the look of a woman who is possessive about her man. I have seen that often."

"What man?"

"I would judge that it is Mr. Dalton," he said. "Mr. Wayne seems unlikely to inspire passion."

"I must consider this," Margaret said. "Mr. Wayne, incidentally, seems eager to see you." She was still not certain how well the archduke grasped the scope of their plans for his land—the bait they needed to lure the hapless trout who were hungry for quick profit.

The archduke smiled wryly. "He has some idea that he ought to have a title conferred by me."

"Ah," Margaret said. "No doubt he is thinking of a dukedom."

"Not technically possible," he said. "But I did not discourage his ambitions. He was eager to contribute to our cultural fund. I was trying to decide what I might do for him.

There are several minor honorary titles open. I could do more if my country and authority were restored, but that seems some years off.''

The archduke finished off his meal, emptied his wine glass, and beamed with satisfaction. "I hope it comes in my life-time, but then it may only come in the time of my heirs.''

Margaret was amazed, once again, by the ability of human beings to maintain comforting, self-deluding fictions.

"It is much to be wished, sir," she said, "for you to regain your rightful place. I am now going to be very im-proper in proposing a business arrangement between us.''

Archduke Niklas looked at her warily. "In spite of what you might have heard, my dear," he said finally, "I am not at all wealthy. I made that clear to Emma from the start. Once I had cleared up her misapprehensions, she and I be-came partners of a sort.''

"Good heavens, it's nothing to do with money," Margaret said. "It is the management of your worthless, useless land. . . .''

"Suitable only for mirages," he said.

"Yet this fantasy land—merely the idea that it exists—has a significant value to Dalton and his friends. I believe it must be tied to Emma's murder, and might be dangerous to you. I would like to have you agree to declare to one and all that only I will make the final decision about the land. This is not to say," she added quickly, "that I am asking that the power of decision be taken from you. I merely wish for the appearance of complete authority.''

"You want them to think that you control it. I see.'' The archduke put his old thin hand to his forehead and thought. "They are a devilish crowd," he said. "I agree to your pro-posal. All I wanted was a bit of ready money to take me to the sun for my final years.'' He sighed.

"We still might manage that," Margaret said. "But I wish to make certain that you do have years to look forward to.''

"You will be in the same peril that struck Emma down?''

"I can take care of myself," Margaret said. "I will be prepared where she was not.''

They strolled easily back toward Margaret's apartment

building. There was little traffic on the streets and the car owners who had been fortunate enough to find legal parking spaces had put their vehicles to bed at the curbs.

Neither the archduke nor Margaret noticed that a dark-clad figure on the opposite side of the street kept pace with them as they chatted in the cool night.

As they reached Margaret's building, she said, "May I ask an impertinent question?"

The archduke, mellow in the glow of a good dinner with good wine, nodded his regal assent.

"Might I ask if Emma ever purchased socks for you?"

"Socks? Stockings?" The archduke was puzzled. "Yes, she did. They were a bargain, she said. Not the right sort, alas, but I could not bring myself to tell her. She was so pleased with herself."

The silent figure across the street from the building watched the doorman bow the archduke into the lobby and hasten to summon the elevator for him and Margaret.

Chapter 13

The next morning, Marcus was sent pedaling off to United National Bank & Trust to pick up the material Dalton had given to Paul, and Margaret ventured blearily out into a misty morning to the Villa d'Este hotel for a breakfast she did not care to consume.

Tina was already seated at a table draped in pink linen with a modest spray of pinkish orchids in a crystal vase at the center. The table commanded a superior view of the Trevi Room. And yes, there was a fountain, although not quite on the scale of its namesake in Rome.

Most of the tables were taken by freshly barbered businessmen who put their heads together to talk of deals that reeked of dollar signs. Margaret half expected to see Yale Dalton and Wayne D. Wayne lurking behind the massed greenery at the perimeter of the room, but they were not in evidence.

"You are quite amazing, Tina," Margaret said. She took pains to view her in light of the archduke's comments.

"What do you mean?" Tina said. She too looked very businesslike today, in a gray pinstripe suit and a white blouse, although Margaret noted that the skirt was short to show off her good legs and the jacket was nipped in to show off her narrow waist.

"You look like a new person every time I see you."

"I think people of necessity play a number of roles," Tina said. "But we are the same underneath."

"I suppose that kind of consistency helps us to maintain our equilibrium when business, for example, requires us to pretend we are not deeply attached to a person who means a great deal."

Tina didn't blink, but Margaret wondered if she had caught her meaning.

"I heard that Wayne D. Wayne would like to play the role of titled gentleman," Margaret said.

Tina—not often amused in Margaret's experience—laughed heartily. "What a fool that man can be. Oh, yes. He found out that an acquaintance back home, or more likely some old rival, had acquired the right to be called 'Lord of the Manor' or some such nonsense, merely by having sufficient cash to buy it. So he's been trying to negotiate with the so-called archduke. How would you know about that?"

"The archduke himself told me. He's staying with me now. Didn't you know?"

"No. I'd heard that he'd gone from his place." She caught herself. "I mean to say, he hasn't been answering his phone. We've been trying to reach him."

Margaret knew there was no telephone, so the Dalton-Wayne crowd must have come knocking again at the dusty old apartment on Riverside Drive, and had been disappointed.

"We have family ties that go back years and years," Margaret said. "He was so distressed by Emma Ross's death that I didn't think it right to leave him alone. Now he's asked me to take charge of all his business affairs. I really don't know much about such matters, but my good common sense will see us through." Margaret hoped she sounded both dim enough to take Tina in and clear enough about her role so there would be no mistake. There was none.

Tina said, "Well, as long as you've taken him in hand, there were some financial matters pending when Emma died. Perhaps the archduke hasn't had time to explain everything, but some land of his plays a small part in a project we're working on. Not essential by any means, but Emma had agreed to certain terms."

"Yes, the land has been mentioned. What was it? I'm such a *silly*, forgetful person." Margaret enjoyed playing the flighty aristocrat, and only hoped she was convincing Tina. "But that's the problem I mentioned. I did agree to work with Yale, but now that the archduke has asked me to assist, I'd hate to find myself involved in a conflict of interest. It's all so *terribly* confusing."

"Emma had no problem in a similar relationship," Tina said.

"Yes, but she was murdered," Margaret said, trying to sound uneasy. "I still can't believe it. To think that you were all right there and never thought to look about for her."

Tina's expression did not change, but Margaret saw the faintest tightening about her mouth. "There were several other guests when we arrived," she said.

That was wrong, Margaret knew, if the archduke was to be believed.

"In any event," Margaret said, "I wouldn't feel right about introducing Yale to . . . to prospective investors. I mean to say, I do know people. . . . You yourself have met that nice Italian boy." Margaret looked for a telltale blush, a hint that the always devastating charm of Paul had touched Tina Corrado.

Tina merely smiled. "Prince Paul is quite a likable young man," she said.

"I'm *so* glad you hit it off the other night. Should I ask if there's a possibility of a romance? And you must tell me if he plans to invest all those spare Castrocani *lire* in some good sound American business."

"I enjoy his company," Tina said, "but I don't know about his investment plans. You would have to ask Yale. And I would not worry about a conflict in working with him. I should say that managing the archduke's affairs might well be part of your work with Yale. Our investors like to be assured that everything is in order.

"We have had considerable success so far, and for some of our enterprises, the early investors have already received substantial profits. We'd naturally want to use your name to enhance our position. Titles can be rather attractive to the sort of people we're interested in.''

"I had no idea," Margaret said, knowing quite well the power of her name in certain circles. "Kenny Smith had a similar idea about my name and title to help promote his undertakings.''

"Kendall can be difficult," Tina said. "He's obsessed with this clothing line he's preparing to spring on unsuspecting women of not much taste. Are you attending his little show?''

"He hasn't mentioned it. I know only of his book party.''

"It's a test run during lunch at some half-fashionable restaurant," Tina said. "Emma made him some rash promises. It was done without reference to Yale.''

"I didn't imagine Yale would be interested in couture," Margaret said. "Although I do know that Marie d'Avalon is.''

Tina jerked her head up from the tiny muffin she was smearing with a very small trace of butter. "People are always trying to interest our group in their harebrained schemes. We have little to do with that woman.''

"I've got it wrong, then," Margaret said. Lies, lies, and more lies. "I understood that Avalon Hills referred to her. And since Marie is advising Kenny, and since Kenny seems to be part of your overall scheme . . .''

"*Only* peripherally," Tina said firmly.

"Then perhaps it was Belinda Hope who put Yale onto the possibilities of the fashion market for the masses. He's such an attractive man that I can just see all these women finding good reason to be close to him.''

Tina's mouth was a tight line now. Margaret seemed to have hit a raw nerve. If Tina was more than Yale's little ol' administrator, possibly she was not pleased about Yale's morning visits to the Hope apartment. "The Hopes are business acquaintances," she said. "Norman has invested very wisely with us." She was all business again. "His participation and the old man's willingness to sell certain lands are somewhat related.''

"You mean *my* willingness to have him sell," Margaret

said. "I'm planning to go through all the papers Emma left behind."

Tina looked at her. "I thought you would have done that," she said.

Margaret felt the tiniest clutch of nerves. They did know, then, that she was the one who found the stolen portfolio and had returned it anonymously. Well, it was too late to worry, and she had laid out just about every hint she could manage about what she knew or surmised about the relationships among everyone involved with Emma, alive and dead.

"I've seen some things of Emma's, of course," Margaret said bravely, "but I've really been too distressed about the murder to think clearly. We don't know who killed her, do we? Why, it could have been just about anyone."

"I doubt that," Tina said. She was looking beyond Margaret now to the entrance to the Trevi Room. At last, Yale Dalton and Wayne D. Wayne were hovering at the maitre d's station.

While Margaret braced for their arrival, which seemed imminent, she found that she herself was doubting her own words about Emma. It really could *not* have been just anyone. She remembered something Marcus had said about his delivery, and what Emma had been wearing when the body was discovered.

"Look who's here to brighten a gray old mornin'," Yale said heartily. "Is our little Tina takin' good care of you?"

"Yes, certainly," Margaret said. She had noticed the hand he placed on Tina's shoulder, Tina's almost involuntary look of pleasure, the momentary intimate exchange of looks. The archduke was not far wrong. "Tina has been most enlightening, and I might say, persuasive about me linking up with your group in a number of ways."

"Lady Margaret has taken over management of Archduke Niklas's affairs," Tina said. "I thought you'd like to fill her in on details of the Development."

"Now that might be a little premature," Wayne said, but at a sharp look from Dalton he drew back.

"I'd be glad to hear *all* about everything someday soon," Margaret said. "And you can explain what it is you'd like from dear Nicky.'' Margaret was bred to formality; the nickname didn't come easily, but she wanted her standing with the archduke to be clear. ''I don't have the time today, as I'm needed by Mr. Kasparian.''

''Tonight?'' Yale said. ''Tomorrow?''

''I'm totally booked today and tomorrow, although I do hope to drop by the Kendall Smith show of his new line tomorrow at lunch. We'll arrange something very soon.''

Margaret wanted now to get away and think about the idea that had blossomed in the midst of sparring with Tina. She had the beginning of an idea about who had done Emma in, but scarcely a clue as to why.

''I'll ring you,'' she said to the group in general, ''the instant I have a free moment.''

When a quick exit was required, Margaret excelled. She had gathered her handbag and departed before another word was said.

Chapter 14

*B*edros Kasparian looked up from his desk at the far end of the elegant, narrow shop. "Well, well," he said benevolently, "it is Tuesday as I predicted, and you have finally found time for my poor enterprise. Mrs. Phillip Courtney will be in at eleven, so you will be useful to make some small talk while I persuade her to purchase something very expensive. She will like the special Ming vase very much, but would find it far too costly if I show it first. Even after she has seen everything, and is certain the Ming is a bargain, she will hesitate, and I will be required to take her to lunch. These eager but inexperienced collectors are difficult."

"I was planning to be out around midday," Margaret said.

"Still tracking down the murderer?" He shook his head. "That sort of thing could be dangerous."

"It isn't exactly a matter of tracking anyone down," Margaret said. "It's a matter of reviewing various possibilities."

"In any event," Kasparian said, "I didn't plan to have you join us. Mrs. Courtney likes titles, but is not overly fond of the company of women much younger than she."

"Ah, well. If she likes titles, she'll be happy to meet a friend who plans to stop by. An elderly gentlemen with a grand title. He may pretend to be buying, but he is without funds, so you need not have your expectations raised."

"A gentleman with a lofty title who has some involvement

118

in a recent murder, perhaps? Margaret, you are incorrigible.''

''Archduke Niklas is staying with me for a few days. He doesn't have much to occupy himself, so I thought he might enjoy a visit to an important Madison Avenue shop that specializes in Oriental antiques. He is a true innocent. . . .'' And as she spoke the words, she decided that innocence was the wrong word for the archduke. He had the simplicity of an old man who had put a complicated life behind him, but he was not an innocent.

''Why would you take a *faux* archduke under your wing, dear Margaret? Has he no retinue of his own?''

''His 'retinue' is dead, Kasparian, and I am somewhat worried about his safety. There are doubtful characters circling around him, and there are suspicious dealings about land that is worthless and promises that are golden. Not to mention a line of expensive clothes, a beauty spa, a few empty titles for sale, and conceivably several sordid romances. I am simply holding off the tide until I can figure out who did Emma in.''

''The police,'' Kasparian said firmly, ''remain better equipped to make such a determination. They must have suspects.''

The gentle chime of the doorbell signaled the arrival of Marcus, the principal suspect. Marcus looked at fierce bronze temple guardians bearing swords and wearing elaborate headdresses artfully lighted in wall niches. He gazed at the golden Japanese kimono on the wall, the T'ang camel, the Noh masks.

''Nice,'' he said. ''That guy went around to the apartment on Park a few minutes ago, same as yesterday. I watched him go in and then I came here with this from the bank.'' He handed Margaret a packet.

''Kasparian, this is my colleague, Marcus, who is the center of police attention but is definitely not the perpetrator. Marcus, this is Bedros Kasparian, who is my employer and friend.''

Kasparian nodded warily. Marcus looked at him from his comparatively great height and said, ''Right.''

"Since Marcus is on my payroll," Margaret said, "and I have no immediate tasks for him, is there any little errand you need done swiftly and efficiently?"

Kasparian hesitated. "Goldblum has two Hokusai woodcuts he wants me to sell on consignment. Mr. . . . um . . . Marcus might fetch them? Safely? He's uptown at Ninety-second Street."

"Excellent," Margaret said. "I'll get the address, and Marcus will see that the pictures are delivered safely back here. They're rather valuable, Marcus, so take special care."

When Marcus had departed, Kasparian frowned. "Is this wise, Margaret? What do we know of him?"

"Nothing really," Margaret said, "but he is not a murderer."

"I was thinking more along the lines of a thief."

"If he steals the Hokusais, you'll have to take their cost from my commissions," she said cheerfully. "Although it might take quite awhile to pay them off. Ah, the archduke makes his entrance."

She opened the door to the archduke in his cape and a broad-brimmed felt hat. He carried a gold-handled walking stick.

"Before I introduce you," Margaret said quickly, "do you know what has become of the contents of Emma's apartment?"

"There was so little," the archduke said. "A few small cartons are to be sent around. I did not take furniture."

"I see," Margaret said. "Come along and meet Bedros Kasparian."

"I am here merely to look," he said to Kasparian when Margaret introduced them. "Margaret tells me that you have some very fine objects."

"Please, sir . . ." Short, elegant Bedros Kasparian made a sweeping gesture to welcome the tall and threadbare archduke to the shop. "I'd be pleased to show you anything from our stock that might interest you. These bits on display are merely representative. Teasers, don't you know?" The million or so dollars worth of "teasers" displayed about the showroom could easily have fit into the Saks shopping bag where Emma had hidden her treasures.

"I confess my tastes run rather to seventeenth- and eighteenth-century European silver," the archduke said. "And I have a weakness for gems . . . so useful as gifts to lovely ladies to smooth the path to greater delights."

"A circlet of diamonds has a remarkable effect on the feminine spirit," Kasparian said. "Would you have been about Paris in the mid-thirties? I was a young man, just getting started as a dealer, but I seem to recall hearing your name from clients. I dealt in paintings then, the impressionists and the cubists. I was soon to embark on my American adventure, from which I have never managed to be released."

"Perhaps you encountered René Gimpel during your Paris years?" Archduke Niklas asked. "I used to meet him often."

"An extraordinary dealer. And the painters back then were far more interesting chaps than those you encounter today. I used to see Braque about, and Picasso, naturally."

"Picasso, yes. Let me tell you a tale about him that's never been written up," the archduke said as Kasparian guided him toward the back of the shop.

Such a small world, Margaret thought, whatever one's age or origin. Archduke Niklas had made his way to New York via decades in the capital cities of Europe sporting a lofty title and history. Kasparian had made his way from the poverty of Armenia and Turkey to his present eminence as a dealer in antiques catering to the decorating whims of overrich New York society matrons. Along the way, their lives had touched via common acquaintances.

One of Kasparian's superrich ladies appeared now. Mrs. Phillip Courtney was past middle age, but she had deftly managed to evade the crueler depredations of the years. Money was useful in this.

Kasparian abandoned the archduke and hastened to meet his very good customer. The archduke left off his cape and hat and trailed behind him.

"Oh dear," Margaret said aloud. Surely the archduke

would not hinder Kasparian's sales pitch. She was quickly at Kasparian's side.

"You know Lady Margaret Priam, I'm sure," Kasparian said. "And may I present His Highness the Archduke Niklas of . . ." He had no idea of the archduke's claimed territories, but continued smoothly. "But you must already be acquainted. . . ."

Mrs. Courtney said, "We are not, but I am delighted. . . ." Two titles had put roses in her cheeks, unless they could be laid to Estée Lauder's best blusher.

"Madame, I am honored." Niklas almost clicked his heels, almost bowed, and raised Mrs. Courtney's hand to his lips and almost kissed it. "I have longed for the opportunity to be introduced. One naturally hears your name spoken in the good circles. I hope I do not intrude if I join you? No? Then shall we take chairs so that Mr. Kasparian can show us some little *objets* that might fit your collection? I am right, am I not, in understanding that you are a dedicated collector?"

"Well, yes, I try to acquire good pieces from time to time, although I confess to being a mere amateur compared with others."

"The archduke," Kasparian said, improvising freely, "has superb taste, and a great eye for value."

"My dear Kasparian," the archduke said as he and Mrs. Courtney settled into comfortable chairs upholstered in Chinese brocade. "Young people like Mrs. Courtney are scarcely interested in an old man's opinion. Still, I have had some experience with buying art."

Margaret was impressed by the skill with which the archduke ingratiated himself with the moneyed classes. All this must seem like old—and better—times.

"I would be honored to have your advice . . . Your Highness," Mrs. Courtney said. "I have such a difficult time deciding. I had an interior designer who tried to guide me, but I fired him. He had no sense at all of who I am and what my rooms must say. He had no sense at all about the spiritual bonds that tie me to the East. How I wish Morley Manton were still in business. He was a tyrant, but he *understood*."

"Lady Margaret will fetch a few small pieces to examine. And there is a stunning white jade bowl that might interest you. I managed to obtain it at auction only last month. Quite rare. I have something rather special that you might care to look at later." Kasparian winked at Margaret, confident that the very rare and expensive Ming vase would soon reside in Mrs. Courtney's townhouse.

As Margaret departed for the rooms behind the showroom where the artworks were stored, she heard the archduke say, "But dear lady, Monte Carlo has become so declassé. Tennis players live there now. And musicians. Deauville, which I knew well as a young man, is coming back. You *must* consider it."

Mrs. Courtney, doubtless burdened with more money than sense, replied, "I had heard that, but you would know better than I, sir."

"Niklas, please. The time has passed when we must stand on ceremony especially with friends."

"Genevieve," Mrs. Courtney said, and the Estee Lauder blush deepened.

The old devil, Margaret thought. She knew she had witnessed the greatest treasure Archduke Niklas, whoever he was, had to share: pure golden charm. When she returned bearing the pieces, Kasparian was settled back in his chair, nodding and smiling, and listening to the archduke ramble on about titled persons and glamorous places and mighty empires risen and fallen. Mrs. Courtney was absorbing his every word.

Margaret placed a pale green jade statue of a bird on a deep blue square of velvet and the white bowl on red.

"But these are superb," the archduke said. "I know something of jade, Genevieve, and I would very definitely suggest that you . . ." He paused and looked over at Kasparian, who unobtrusively stretched out a hand seemingly to stretch fingers a bit cramped by age. Two percent of the price to the archduke if she bought. Then a raised finger indicating there was more to come.

The archduke said, "Both are definitely worth your consideration. We will decide after we have seen what other *objets* Mr. Kasparian has to offer.''

Margaret wondered if she would lose her job to a sharp old schemer. Then Kasparian looked at Margaret with a bland smile, and she was reassured that the archduke would have his commission, but she would have her job.

By the time the archduke had finished working his wonders with Mrs. Courtney, she had committed herself to the jade bird, the white bowl, and a lovely celadon plate. She was seriously considering the nearly priceless Ming vase, a beautiful piece eight inches high, a quadrangle with a square mouth and decorated with dragons, birds, fruit, and flowers in five colors. Margaret always held her breath when carrying it, since it would take literally decades and decades of commissions to repay any damage to it. The archduke had accumulated several thousand dollars in commissions from Kasparian, and had also apparently arranged his winter holiday plans. Mrs. Courtney had diffidently asked him to consider spending some weeks at the Courtneys' Palm Beach home during the coming winter.

The archduke, Kasparian, and Mrs. Courtney swept out for an expensive lunch. Margaret thought it was time to reconsider the archduke. Frail perhaps, and certainly old. The grateful recipient of kindness and services. But not helpless by any means. He was about as sharp a dealer as she'd ever encountered.

She wondered if Dalton, Wayne, and Tina had any idea of the person behind Emma, Lady Ross. They were all rank amateurs in comparison. Archduke Niklas was a force to be reckoned with, and if someone thought that by eliminating Emma, obstacles to the grand scheme would vanish, he—or she—was very wrong.

Marcus arrived with the woodcuts safely in hand only minutes after Kasparian and the archduke led Mrs. Courtney away.

''Marcus, I have it in mind to visit the lady on Park Avenue. Do you suppose she is alone by now?''

''Whatever he's doing there, it ain't taking him long,'' Marcus said.

"Then suppose you find a place in the back of the shop and stand guard. The door will be locked and no one will stop by, since Kasparian sees people only by appointment, but it's good to have someone in the place when the alarms aren't rigged. There's usually a boy around, but he doesn't appear to be in."

Marcus shrugged his assent.

"I know antiques aren't as satisfying as baking, but you might like to look at some of the reference books in the back room," she said. "I won't be long."

"This is like some kind of TV cop show," he said, "trailing people and looking at suspects."

"Exactly," Margaret said. "And don't forget who the best suspect is."

"Yeah," Marcus said. "Me."

"Don't worry," she said. "I've come up with a couple of second bests who might replace you. The coat on the chair in Emma's apartment when you delivered the food that night. What was it like?"

"Light-colored," he said. "Brownish."

"Like a trench coat? Man's or woman's?"

"Hey, I didn't touch it, and how would I know? It didn't, you know, look like anything one way or the other."

"We'll know eventually," Margaret said. "Try not to break anything while I'm gone."

Chapter 15

"*Could you* announce to Mrs. Hope that Lady Margaret Priam would like to come up?"

The apartment building on Park Avenue was richly silent, the doorman's uniform was well tailored, the splatter of autumn rain that had begun to fall was not allowed to sully the marble floor.

Margaret longed to quiz the doorman about Yale Dalton's morning visits, but she knew that if the annual Christmas gift was substantial enough, and if the occupants were reasonably pleasant year-round, doormen at this level of real estate were not free with gossip to strangers.

"I do not know if she is in, ma'am," the doorman said. "She may have gone out to lunch, as is her habit. I only just came on duty."

Lunch is the great time-filler, Margaret thought. Not much else for the Belinda Hopes of the world to do, except roam the department stores and boutiques and have one's hair done.

But Margaret was in luck. Belinda hadn't yet departed for her delicate quenelles and leafy salad with barely enough calories to sustain life as we know it.

"I was on the point of leaving," Belinda said. "I can manage to be a bit late, but not *too* late." She was made up and dressed up, ready to be the envy of her luncheon partners.

"I'll only take a minute or two," Margaret began.

Belinda allowed her to enter a vast drawing room in which a decorator had drawn his inspiration from a vision of an English country house, or better, a Ralph Lauren shop, to judge from the amount of dark wood, chintz, leather, and rural-looking knicknacks in evidence.

"It's a committee luncheon for Kenny's fête," Belinda said. "No one's done much work besides me, but it's useful to have some good names connected with the thing. I don't expect to make any money, but no matter, Kenny's paying for everything. He's simply dying to be famous. Not only clothes, but everything. A lifestyle."

"Starting with the divine little Kenny Smith boutiques, I take it," Margaret said. "And of course, there's always Kenny: The Fragrance."

Margaret sat on a puffy sofa upholstered in cabbage roses and rapidly sank deep into the soft cushion.

"And the book. Nobody ever *started* with a book. That usually comes later. I believe this party will get some important publicity. I'm hoping *Vanity Fair* will photograph it. Masquerades are great fun, don't you think? And all those feathery costumes people will be wearing. I see it as a real news story." She paused. "Although I do hope we won't have any trouble with the animal rights people. I mean, feathers aren't like fur."

"Only if you are not a bird," Margaret said. "Yes, I am sure it will be great fun." Since Margaret had little interest in dressing up to appear other than she was, she could not express sincere enthusiasm for attending a party looking like The Dying Swan or Chicken Little. And she imagined the horror that would wash over De Vere's face if she ever suggested that he don fancy dress, let alone that which included feathers.

"Margaret, I've just had a *grand* idea. I know it's late in the day to ask, and I can't promise there's still time to get your name printed on the program and so forth, but you *must* be on my committee. Your name, the title—a genuine title—would add such glamour and dignity."

"I really can't accept," Margaret said. Everyone seemed

to have plans to market themselves via the title that was an accident of birth in the first place, and basically only of value in getting a reservation at a difficult restaurant.

Belinda looked disappointed for a fraction of a second, but recovered admirably. "Now tell me why it is that you stopped by."

"One or two things," Margaret said. "I happened to be in the neighborhood, and I needed advice about Kenny's party, actually. I have *no* idea what to wear. I'm not clever about costumes. What are you wearing?"

"I wasn't going to mention it to anyone," Belinda said, "but I've almost decided to appear as a Ziegfeld show girl, all those fabulous feathers on my head and quite a sexy little outfit with lots and lots of sequins. On the other hand, there's always Marie Antoinette with a big, big gown and a powdered wig and big, big feathers on my head."

"It must be a trial to decide," Margaret said.

"You ought to get Kenny's advice. He has *such* imagination."

"Poor Emma would have enjoyed it," Margaret said carefully, finally bringing the conversation around to the subject she wanted to discuss. Yes, there was a slight grimace at the mention of Emma's name. "I still can't believe that anyone would murder her," Margaret continued, "I do know that she tended to . . . well, flirt a bit, but she was harmless."

"That is your opinion."

Margaret feigned horror and embarrassment. "Belinda dear, I'm *so* sorry. I'd quite forgotten the business with Norman. But no one took it seriously, and I do understand how erring husbands can drive one to . . . other comforts. I do think Yale Dalton is quite attractive in a simple, rough-hewn way."

Belinda was becoming annoyed. She twisted the Important Daytime Ring on her long-nailed finger. "We don't know the man well. Norman is engaged in some business or other with him. I have nothing to do with him."

"Now that's the other thing I wanted to ask. You said very plainly at Emma's party that you didn't know Yale, but I have heard ever so many rumors about a very close relationship. Why do you suppose people are saying that?''

"I don't care what people say," Belinda said, controlling a very real fury.

"I didn't mean to suggest . . ." Margaret paused. "I think he would be the perfect escort for me to Kenny's party. I'm rather working with him, did you know?"

"I didn't," Belinda said shortly. She stood up. Margaret had been wondering how long she would tolerate this bitchy nonsense, even from a titled English lady. "I really must leave."

"Before you go, I'm curious to know why Wayne pushed Norman overboard the other night. It seems like such a childish thing to do. But then I was thinking, suppose it had something to do with Norman's affair with Emma? Or something to do with Yale? Or perhaps something to do with Emma's murder?"

"He fell," Belinda said. "He was not pushed. And no matter what that clod Wayne says, *it had nothing to do with anyone!*" Belinda turned around suddenly as she was proceeding toward the door. "I *hope* you don't think *I* had anything to do with Emma's death."

"It crossed my mind that it was likely she was done in by a woman."

"It certainly was *not* me. If you're looking for a woman to accuse, I suggest you take a look at Marie d'Avalon or that girl Tina. They're both no better than they should be."

"I remember you saying just the other day that you thought Marie was so glamorous." Margaret wished that Belinda would break down and confess that she knew both Marie and Tina were rivals for Yale Dalton's affections, and so was Emma, but no such revelations were forthcoming.

Instead, Belinda said, "It turns out Emma put Norman in a rather troublesome position businesswise. If his deals fall through because of some unfounded promises . . ." Belinda flung open the door and waited for Margaret to leave.

"Do take a coat for the rain," Margaret said. "It seems that autumn is upon us today."

"Damn, rain does terrible things to my hair, and I loathe umbrellas. The doorman will get me a cab."

"I'll be seeing you at Kenny's book fête," Margaret said, "with my feathers on."

Margaret telephoned Kasparian's shop. There was no answer. She hoped Marcus hadn't taken it into his head to abscond with the pretty ivory statue of Kuan-yin, which was worth about twelve thousand dollars, or even the gritty-looking little three-legged bronze Shang bowl, which was worth a good deal more.

Instead of returning to Kasparian's, Margaret went around to Emma's building. There was a discernible difference between it and the building where the Hopes lived. The lobby cried for a paintbrush, the floor was scuffed, and the doorman noticeably truculent. Margaret supposed it signified the difference between a co-op building with apartments in the millions and one with ten floors of studios and two-and-a-half-room apartments, all with finite leases and high rents.

"The super? He's in the office," the doorman said, "but Harry don't like to be bothered in the afternoon. If you're here about renting the apartment where the lady got murdered, it's not being shown yet."

"I'm not looking for an apartment," Margaret said, "only Harry."

The building super might have been dismissed as a suspect, but he looked a lot meaner than Marcus. He was almost asleep behind a cluttered desk in a room crammed with odd pieces of furniture looted from vacated apartments. The aroma of very modestly priced whiskey hovered about him like a cloud, and the buttons on his plaid shirt strained to contain his ample stomach.

"Hullo? Hullo?" Margaret trilled. "So sorry to trouble you."

Harry's eyelids lifted briefly and fell, and he gurgled deep in his chest. Then he shook his head, opened his eyes, and attempted to focus on Margaret.

"Whaddya want? You a tenant?"

"I am . . . I was a friend of Lady Ross. I have come to fetch the contents of her apartment."

Harry heaved himself to his feet. "I got murder, I got cops, I got all kinds of trouble, and you think I got time to pack up her stuff? Anyhow, they said they didn't want the furniture. They said I could have it."

"Who are 'they'?"

"The cops. They said the old guy, her grandfather or whoever he was, wanted the stuff in the drawers and closets, but not the furniture."

"Is it packed up?"

"Yeah," Harry conceded. "It took me and Lopez a couple of hours, and I don't get paid for doing that."

"I'll see that you're paid for your trouble," Margaret said. "Where are Emma's things?"

"In the basement, in a coupla boxes."

"Then we'll go to fetch them, shall we?"

"Who the hell did you say you are?"

"A friend of Lady Ross and the old gentleman. He asked me to come around. You must remember me. I was with Detective De Vere of the New York police the night she was murdered." She removed from her pocket a substantial-looking roll of twenty-dollar bills to goad him to action.

"I remember now. You know the cops brought me in and acted as if I killed that little tramp? Lady Ross she called herself. I seen her kind plenty of times. It just so happened I got back from being in White Plains all day right when the cops were pulling up. No way they could pin it on me. I oughta sue for false arrest, get a big settlement."

"You weren't actually arrested," Margaret said, "so I don't think you can sue. About Emma's possessions."

"There's the back rent that's got to be paid. She was a month behind."

"Surely there was a security deposit," Margaret said, "and if that doesn't cover it, the building's owners can deal with her estate. Besides, you have the furniture to sell."

"Wasn't much, and not good stuff."

"Nevertheless. Shall we go to the basement?"

"Just a lot of junk," he muttered, and shuffled past her,

keeping his eye on the money in her hand. He led her down some dark stairs into the basement. An eerie tangle of pipes and wires covered the ceiling. Margaret was certain she saw a long-dead mouse in a corner.

"That's all there is," Harry said. Two taped-up cartons were stacked beside the door to the furnace room.

"Is there someone to help me get these into a cab?" Margaret said. She was disappointed. The boxes were small, less than two feet square. She'd hoped for something more.

"Lopez, you lazy son of a bitch," Harry shouted as he stuffed Margaret's money into his pocket. "Wake up and help the lady."

A slight man with a broom came around a corner.

"Get this stuff upstairs, Lady Ross's things. Move it." Harry shuffled away to his lair without looking back.

Lopez picked up both cartons. "No problem," he said. "You want all her things? You taking the bag, too?"

"What bag would that be?"

"Over there."

A large green trash bag stuffed full rested far back in the shadows.

"Is clothes from the bedroom, the closets," Lopez said. "She's not a bad lady, you know. The boss kinda like her, but she wasn't giving him any time."

"I think I can manage the bag," Margaret said, "if you take the boxes. No, she wasn't bad, Mr. Lopez. She was just a dreamer like the rest of us."

Chapter 16

Margaret had her taxi wait while she dashed into Kasparian's shop. She found him and Archduke Niklas back from lunch with Mrs. Courtney. The three of them hovered over yet another jade piece. They were suspiciously jolly, as though a celebratory glass of wine or two had toasted Mrs. Courtney's latest additions to her collection.

"I shan't be staying, if that's all right," Margaret said. "And if Marcus is still about, I'll be taking him with me."

"Enjoy your murders," Kasparian said airily.

Marcus was in the back, leafing through a thick illustrated book about ancient Chinese ceremonial bronzes.

"You got someplace for me to go?" he asked.

"Yes, to my place. Have you been bored?"

He shook his head. "I kinda like it back here." Marcus waved his hand around at the shelves loaded with priceless treasures of the East resting in lacquered and silk-covered boxes. "Besides," he said, "it was raining outside last I looked."

"I have a cab outside. You can leave the bicycle here. Come along."

Between the two of them, they carried Emma's boxes and the bag of clothing up to Margaret's apartment.

"Open the boxes and see what we have," she said. "I want a look at what's in here." She tore open the plastic

133

trash bag and dumped out the contents on the floor. There was Emma's pretty lingerie, a couple of dresses and a suit, two pairs of shoes, a few rather nice sets of sheets and pillow slips, and two coats. One, a tailored black lightweight wool, carried the faint scent of perfume. The other was a light beige, cut full with raglan sleeves, a belt rather than buttons, and no label. There was nothing in the pockets, nothing to indicate whether it was a man's coat or a woman's.

Margaret tried it on. Since she was fairly tall, it was a bit shorter than she liked. The sleeves seemed a little long, but they had been turned back. She was almost certain that she had seen this coat, or something very like it, in the closet the night Emma had been murdered, when Margaret went to fetch the archduke's cape.

It was proof of nothing, of course, but it gave Margaret an idea of what could have transpired: someone came to see Emma before the party, wearing the coat, and had left it on the chair where Marcus had seen it. He or she had strangled her, found the old note to the archduke, hung the coat in the closet, and departed before the archduke arrived first, by his own admission. The murderer returned later coatless as a guest—and that meant it could be anyone, from one of the Dalton gang to the very last arrival.

It sounded good.

"Marcus, look at this." She modeled the coat, belt loosely tied, collar up. "Do you remember it?"

He frowned. "You want me to say it's the coat on the chair, right?"

"That's up to you."

"It might be. Close to it."

Margaret told him her idea.

"I see," Marcus said, "but why leave the coat behind?"

"Oh, perhaps to look different each time the person came in."

"There's a doorman. Usually. A guy was there when I brought the food from Navets Nouveaux, but sometimes no one's around. And, like there's guys that know me, and they send me up and don't even ring that I'm coming."

"If the person—the murderer—was someone who came

often," Margaret said slowly, "maybe the doorman would pay no attention, or forget this person was a visitor, and think it was a tenant."

"Or . . ." Marcus was pleased with another idea. "If you got in without the doorman seeing you, you could go around the corner to the stairs, up one flight and catch the elevator there. No hanging around to be noticed. You come down the same way, wait until nobody was around and leave."

"Going up to Emma's party was certainly no problem that night. I was just waved in," Margaret said.

Margaret sighed and sorted out some of the other items that had been dumped from the trash bag. Marie's borrowed gown was naturally not there, but there were odds and ends of clothing, slips and scarves, and a short wispy tuniclike garment in pale green, trimmed in darker green feathers.

"Now this might be part of the costume Emma planned to wear to Kendall Smith's masquerade party. I wonder what she was supposed to be. Anything of interest in those boxes?"

"Dishes and stuff. Some papers. Drawings."

Margaret took a look. Someone—Kenny probably—had sketched out costumes for Emma.

"Marcus, I'm getting tired. Only a week ago I had a life that had nothing to do with Emma Ross and her people. I have a lovely man friend that I haven't been seeing, and there are all my other friends, who have nice dinner parties and houses in the country to visit. There are books to be read and plays to be seen. Instead I'm digging around trying to find out what silly fantasy of Emma's triggered a reason to kill her."

"Hey," Marcus said. "You ain't telling me what I don't know. Different, but . . . I have a girl." He stopped. "I used to have a girl, but she doesn't want to be with someone in trouble with the police. There was old Pierre, with his *sucre* and *beurre* and the bread in the oven. That's gone. Boys I know all my life from the neighborhood suck up crack like it's candy and they die. And some girl down the block—we grew up together—she got three babies and welfare people around looking at her. Man, you think *you* tired. I'm tired.

What kind of big thing is it this woman gets killed? Nothing.''

"But it is something, Marcus," Margaret said. "If only because they picked you first as the guilty party. And then because I don't think it's right that since you didn't do it, they don't bother to find out who did."

"Yeah," Marcus said, "okay. I hope you find the one who did it. She was all right, and the old man too. And the boss."

"The boss?"

"Mr. Kasparian asked if I was not 'otherwise employed for the next month,' would I work around the shop. Some expensive things are being shipped in."

"Ah, well. You would be sort of a bodyguard for the remains of the ancient East. Rather what you said you liked."

"If you need me, I could have time, he said."

"The least he could allow, since I am determined to keep you out of prison for murder," Margaret said. "Don't worry, ducks, I promise they won't hang you." She unfolded the copies she had made of the blueprints found in Yale Dalton's portfolio. "What do you think of this?"

Marcus looked at the plans and shrugged. "I don't know what that stuff is. I saw those kind of things when I was a kid when they let me hang around construction sites, but I don't understand them."

"Well, look," Margaret said, "these must be houses along the roads, and these might be apartment buildings. This looks like a shopping mall, and here's another one. This might be an arena for athletics." She showed him some elevations of buildings with trees, people, and cars drawn in to show the scale. "It's a city, a whole brand new city."

Marcus looked more closely at the plans. "Where they supposed to be building this?" he asked finally.

"I think it's to be away in the desert out west," Margaret said. "On a big piece of land the archduke owns."

"He going to make a lot of money out of this?"

"Not a lot, I'm afraid, or he wasn't going to until I decided I would do the bargaining for him."

"Yeah, and who's building it?"

"Yale Dalton, the one who visits the lady on Park Avenue.

I should say, he's telling people about it so they'll invest a lot of their money to pay for it.''

"Huh." Marcus was not impressed. "These are the plans? Then it's a fake. They'll take the money and disappear, and there won't be any city."

"Why do you say that?" Margaret felt that this would be the case in the end, but she had no basis for her suspicions.

"Where's the highways?" Marcus asked. "How you goin' to get to this city? And there ain't no airport."

Margaret smiled. "Why, thank you, Marcus. You are absolutely right."

When Marcus went back to Kasparian, promising to remind the archduke to make his way back to Margaret, she called Dianne Stark.

"Two questions," Margaret said. "Could you ask Charlie if he's heard any talk of a development called Avalon Hills and . . ."

"First question first," Dianne said. "He actually mentioned it the other day, when the story of Norman Hope falling overboard was making the rounds. It seems Norman lined up a number of investors for this Avalon Hills thing who are beginning to feel nervous. Charlie's not involved. He's too rich and too smart for that kind of scheme."

"Second question, then," Margaret said. "What's the word on Kenny Smith's party?"

"I really hate to admit it, Margaret, but we're going."

"Really? I never dreamed it was going to be that good."

"It sounded such fun, dress up and all that, and several rather important people seem to be attending. Some are doubtless Kenny's clients, since he does dress a number of high-profile women, although he's become a little too avant-garde for me. And I do like doing something for animals and wildlife."

"In spite of the ostensible beneficiary of this fête," Margaret said, "you will be expected to wear feathers."

"There must be *faux* feathers by this time," Dianne said, "there's *faux* everything else. And there's always chickens. Chickens aren't endangered yet."

"Then what will you wear?"

"I was thinking of making do with a slinky black dress and one of those fancy masks with a few whirls of feathers," Dianne said. "I'll watch everyone else making fools of themselves. What about you?"

"I was thinking along your lines, although I might run around to Kenny and see what he suggests."

"He'd probably be glad to run you up something in ostrich for a few thousand. Oh, won't the incorrigible showoffs be in their glory? Remember the Thurn und Taxis party a couple of years ago at their castle? Lord Glenconner's thing in the Caribbean? I know a lot of the worst exhibitionists are in jail lately or on their way, but there are always enough unindicted co-conspirators to fill up a ballroom. And did you take a look at where Kenny's holding it? That gloomy old men's club off Fifth Avenue that was just forced to allow women in. I suppose the members clear out for the night while the club makes piles of money from the rental fee. The old boys can have their lunches cheap and the taxes get paid for the year. Are you coming with Sam De Vere? I hope so, although I can't imagine him . . ."

"Don't even try," Margaret said. "I'm thinking that the ideal escort would be Yale Dalton, who would probably have gone with Emma, had she lived to see the day."

"Poor Emma. I feel guilty about her, since I consistently said very unkind things about her," Dianne said. "I understand a delivery boy did it."

"The 'boy' is quite a nice young man, and he hasn't murdered anybody that I know of. It was one of a number of respectable people who ought to know better. It could be Yale Dalton or one of his colleagues in shady activities, since Avalon Hills seems to be involved."

"Didn't you say you were attending Kenny's party with Dalton? Even if he is a murderer?"

"Especially," Margaret said. "I'm obliged to pursue this to the end, for the sake of the one person who deserves a peaceful end to a long and tempestuous life, someplace warm and frivolous. Palm Beach or the Riviera or maybe in his own castle in the desert."

The archduke himself returned late in the afternoon after his day of riotous living and beamed fuzzily at Margaret.

"Genevieve is a very fine woman," he said, "very fine. She ought to have a decoration, don't you think? The orders for women are rather restricted, but I think I could justify the Silver Crane. Distinguished Service to the Crown in Time of War. I feel we are engaged in a constant battle. It's a charming little medallion, quite Eastern in its look, so Genevieve will find it congenial to her tastes. She tells me the Palm Beach house is very large so I will be no trouble at all."

"I'm pleased you have made arrangements," Margaret said, her mind on other matters. She ought to see Norman Hope. He had been luring investors on behalf of Dalton, and was finding himself in trouble. The elimination of Emma might have been expected to permit him to disengage himself from his problems. Or if he were still involved with Emma, and Belinda was making trouble . . .

"I was saying," the archduke said, "that I think I will not dine tonight. Luncheon was quite sufficient, and I find that I am feeling somewhat tired. This will not disturb your plans?"

"Oh, no," Margaret said. "Do rest. There is a little television set in your room, did you notice? I might be going out for a time, but please find anything you need in the kitchen."

"How kind you are," the archduke said. "I have been very fortunate all of my life in finding great friends to help me through difficult times." He bowed slightly, and most graciously, to Margaret and departed toward the guest room down the hall where Margaret had installed him. He paused as he reached the entrance to the hall.

"I do find the television program of this Mr. Donahue quite interesting," he said. "We used to see some quite remarkable things in the old days in Paris and Berlin, but he appears to find people who are willing to talk publicly about the most personal and unusual matters." He shook his head. "Most unusual."

Even as Margaret started to plot a reason to get in touch with Norman Hope, he telephoned her. It took awhile to determine why, but eventually it became clear that Belinda had called him at his office and had suggested that Margaret suspected Norman of all manner of wicked deeds.

"I suspect nothing," Margaret said. "And I never suggested any such thing to your wife."

"Meet me around six this evening in the bar of the United Nations Plaza Hotel," he said. "We must talk before this goes any further. We won't be disturbed by people who know me."

Without knowing what "this" was, she agreed. She had enough reasons of her own to talk without worrying about his.

At six, the bar held a number of foreign-looking gentlemen speaking various tongues, doubtless men of diplomatic status who were attending the General Assembly of the United Nations across the street from the hotel. The mirrored walls reflecting more mirrors enlarged the low-ceilinged room to a kind of infinity.

Norman was already there, sitting in a round red chair at a table against a wall.

Almost before she was seated, Norman said, "I don't know what you've heard, but it's not true."

"Norman, I have heard only the rumors that people pass around, and they're just the usual nonsense."

"Avalon Hills is a wonderful project. It was only that Emma suddenly decided that there was something wrong, and maybe the land wouldn't be available. Title to the land is key to our plans. Banks don't want to hear about *maybe*. Your private investor runs at the least smell of trouble."

"I really don't understand what's going on," Margaret said. "Now that I have taken over the dear archduke's business affairs, I will definitely want to have you explain all about Avalon Hills before I decide what's to be done."

Norman's square and manly jaw dropped. "You? Decide?"

Margaret was unstoppable now. "But surely you should be more concerned about the police looking into your personal relationship with Emma. Crimes of passion or crimes to silence someone are much more appealing to the police mind than white collar crime gone wrong.''

The waitress brought Norman a second martini without him asking, and accepted Margaret's request for a decent chardonnay if there was any to be had.

"What you just said, about deciding," Norman said. "I . . . I assumed that with Emma dead, the archduke would be making his own decisions. Marie said . . .''

"I do *not* think you should rely too much on Marie's word that the land actually belongs to her, or will one day. And you do understand that eventually the police are going to learn that you paid for a very expensive Kendall Smith gown for her, and it was the gown that your former lover Emma was planning to wear the night she was murdered.''

Several pale Norman faces reflected back from the mirrored walls. "How . . . how did you know?''

"I guessed. I heard from Kenny that a man paid for the dress, and even though Marie is seeing Yale Dalton . . .''

Normal wiped his brow, and appeared to be hyperventilating.

Margaret went on serenely. "Even though she is seeing Yale, he is not the type of man to buy frivolities for women who are well able to find other men to pay out the necessary cash.''

"It was only a gift," he said. "There's nothing serious between us.''

"A gift that caused you to be tossed into New York Harbor?''

"No . . . well, there was a little trouble with Wayne. Business. It was stupid," he went on, "to be involved with Emma and Marie. It's not that Belinda hasn't been a good wife and mother. . . .'' Margaret sighed and let him continue.

"They were a different kind of experience for me," Norman said. "Outside of reality.''

"And Avalon Hills was the same kind of fantasy.''

Norman slumped down in the soft chair. "At first I believed I could make really big money. Yale is very convincing. I brought people in. Then it started to come apart. Even if we acquired the land, there won't be a city until they can draw water out of the air. I found out that the Pentagon wouldn't even take it as a gift to drop missiles on. Only some conservation group wants it, for a dollar an acre, or maybe it's a square mile. But we need that land, to keep the investors quiet, until we figure out how to make it work.''

''Norman, did you ever take a close look at the plans?''

He looked at her blankly. ''The plans? Why, yes.''

''And you do think Dalton truly planned a city in the desert, and has only been stopped because there are not insurmountable problems like water?''

''I don't understand you.''

''An astute friend pointed out that there are no highways, no airport built in. Dalton has some fancy blueprints. That's all. He certainly has no intention of building Avalon Hills.''

Norman took a hefty gulp of martini.

''I can't be party to fraud,'' Margaret said. ''Then there is the matter of Emma's murder.''

''I was hoping you would find out who,'' he said. ''You could tell us, warn us. . . .''

''Warn you about what?''

''We could be prepared, all of us. Kenny Smith and Marie and even Dalton. I didn't do it, you know that.''

''Oh, Norman. If I could prove that you murdered Emma, I couldn't warn you, any more than the police would. And if you didn't kill her, there's nothing to worry about.'' Margaret sounded reasonable, and Norman still looked worried.

''I didn't kill her,'' he said. ''And I wasn't still seeing her, no matter what Belinda thinks. Belinda wants me to make a lot of money with Avalon Hills so that she can divorce me with a big, big settlement. That's why I need the land, to get free.''

He sounded so miserable that Margaret almost felt sorry for him, but if she were going to be the archduke's champion, she was taking no prisoners.

''Norman, I told you that fraud is not my game. I'm not going to have the archduke sell his land to your crowd for a meager sum so that you can sell off the fantasy to others.''

''We'll offer him more money,'' Norman said eagerly. ''I

think it could work, someday. They will be able to build a city when they figure out how."

"I don't think you can prove that," Margaret said, "but if you do, I'll see that the archduke plays fair. Remember, though, that he doesn't have forever."

Chapter 17

*M*argaret *was* so sure that Marie d'Avalon would have a ringside table at Kendall Smith's preview of his new ready-to-wear line that she didn't even bother to make a date to lunch with her. That would have caused Marie not to show up so as to avoid Margaret entirely.

The show, such as it was, had begun by the time Margaret reached the restaurant, which had definitely not been chosen for its status in the circles of those who knew where to eat and be seen. It was long and narrow and had a ramp descending from a tiny platform stage at the end of the room.

Margaret spotted Marie d'Avalon immediately, alone at a table near the stage watching a sparse line of strutting models parading sarongs, caftans, skimpy bikinis, transparent robes, and satin lounging outfits—and quite a few feathers. Kenny was showing his resort wear. From the look of it, Margaret felt he had a dim future in the mass market. But one never knew what twists of taste would suddenly infect the public.

There was some polite applause, a few flashbulbs, and a lot of loud music as the models swayed back and forth. Although there were a number of women and a scattering of men in the place, there was no one Margaret knew or even recognized. She plotted a path between the tables until she reached Marie, and sat down without an invitation.

"A bit late for the store buyers to be considering resort

wear, don't you think?'' Margaret said above the music. ''Or will Kendall be stocking his own boutiques, and Blooming-dale's and Saks be damned?''

Marie did not look happy. ''I told Kenny that this show would be a mistake. Yale thought so too, but Yale is not so enthusiastic about Kendall Smith Designs these days. I believe Emma had something to do with organizing this show. She was his public relations person. Hah, such a choice to make for such an important undertaking.''

Margaret looked about the narrow room. ''There don't seem to be many people from the fashion press,'' she said. ''So there will be no comment in the papers, and very few people will ever know that his line is rather . . . naive.''

''He should stick to draping,'' Marie said. ''That he does well.''

''There he is,'' Margaret said. ''Lurking at the edge of the stage. He doesn't look too pleased.''

''I hope his book is better than this,'' Marie said.

''We must talk,'' Margaret said.

''We? Talk? I must leave. This show is too painful, and it doesn't matter what Kendall thinks.''

''Marie, we need to talk about your spa and Avalon Hills. Kenny and Emma and the Hopes. Yale Dalton and the arch-duke.''

''Does that terrrrible old man continue to spread rumors? He is jealous.''

''Come along to my apartment, if you're finished here,'' Margaret said. ''Or we could go to your place, if you prefer.''

''I have extremely important business about the city,'' Marie said, ''if you would care to accompany me. We shall talk then. I warn you, however, that I walk. Exercise is important for beauty.''

Margaret found herself being led about the East Side of Manhattan by Marie as she pursued her extremely important errands, most of which were directly related to enhancing her person or wardrobe.

The first stop was a tiny shop dedicated to the sale of the raw ingredients for beauty preparations. While Marie selected scoops of dried twigs and flagons of viscous liquids, Margaret examined a vat that appeared to be filled with seaweed floating in murky waters. When that ceased to fascinate, she contemplated the walls of the shop, which were lined with rows of stoppered bottles containing essences of flowers or powdered reductions of animals, vegetables, and minerals. A young woman with long, straight black hair and quite remarkable makeup was advising a middle-aged matron on how to mix a preparation that would perform an alchemical transformation of wrinkles about the eye into the skin of a teenager.

"This is all rrrrubbish, of course," Marie said over her shoulder as they left the shop, "but it is the best I can find until I arrange to have my own formulas manufactured."

"About your beauty products . . ." Margaret strode along to keep up with healthy Marie.

"Secrets of beauty handed down to me by my mother," Marie said. "Discoveries handed down from generation to generation by the great ladies who sought out the purity of nature in the woods and glens of the French countryside. . . ."

"But I understood your mother was from a wealthy American family," Margaret said. "From one of the western states."

Marie stopped in the middle of the pavement, disregarding the hindrance to others moving rapidly in both directions. "She was acknowledged to have been a great beauty," she said. "Certainly she had beauty secrets. What does it matter where she found them?"

"And with them charmed your father, the war hero who died for his country? An American also, I understand."

"That wicked old man talks too much. But for him, we would still be rich. He ruined my mother and my family."

"How so?" Margaret was curious to see what tale Marie might spin.

"He stole our land, although I am certain he told you it was a gift of a love-besotted woman with no sense."

"But with a cupboard full of beauty secrets, no doubt. I was given to understand that the land is a comparatively useless piece of desert, and that the decline in your family's wealth had nothing to do with Archduke Niklas. And you know, Marie, you ought not go about suggesting that the archduke might be your father, since there are people who know that he was acquainted with your mother somewhat before World War Two. People—you know how people talk—are going to say that you are thus a number of years over fifty.''

Marie tossed her head angrily and said, ''I despise rumors and gossip. Naturally I am many years younger than fifty, and everyone knows that. The land is something else. He promised to return it to me on his death. I have letters.''

''And I believe the archduke has a deed.''

''Foolish old man, who else is there for him to leave it to now that Emma is dead?'' Marie's smile was cunning. ''So you see? I will be proved right in the end. Come along quickly. I must do something about my hair.''

Margaret followed and hoped that she would not have to endure a lengthy stay in a *palais de coiffeur* while Marie made unreasonable demands on a high-priced hair stylist.

Happily, Marie's thick dark hair was not to receive the attention of a master of difficult tresses. Rather, she was headed for a fast stop at Block Pharmacy on Third Avenue, an establishment noted for its remarkable array of hair ornaments: barrettes, clips, bandeaus, pins, poufs, and almost anything else that could be attached to the head. There was the blaze of rhinestones, the polished elegance of tortoise shell, ribbons of every color and plastic moulded into fanciful figures from bananas to leopards.

Marie peered at the racks of barrettes, and leaned over the counter to look at bows. She fingered silk flowers and examined jeweled combs.

''I do not intend to linger,'' Marie said, ''so choose quickly.'' She held up a silver comb heavily encrusted with purple rhinestones in the shape of a bunch of grapes.

''I seldom decorate my hair,'' Margaret said. She was watching two expensively dressed Oriental ladies who seemed to be accompanied by bodyguards. ''I am ready to depart when you are.''

"I must look at some shoes," Marie said.

Margaret's patience was growing thin, but she steeled herself as she moved on to the next store to watch Marie try on a dozen pairs of very costly shoes with extravagantly high heels and plenty of toe cleavage.

"How gracious of Yale Dalton to pay tribute to your relationship by naming the development after you," Margaret said.

"I do not understand what you are saying about a relationship," Marie said. Then she pointed to a shop girl. "You there, find me a pair of these in red." She turned back to Margaret. "Yale Dalton and I are merely friends and business associates. He is backing my spa, as you probably know since you put your pink English nose into everything, just the way Emma did."

Margaret was untouched by her effort to be insulting. "I only ask because of Yale's current affair with Belinda Hope, and with Emma as well, before her death. I have not decided about his relationship with Tina Corrado."

Margaret seemed to have scored with this. Marie reddened and kicked aside the alligator pumps she had been about to try on.

"This place tires me," Marie said, "and I have a pressing engagement elsewhere."

In seconds she had gathered her parcels and departed, leaving Margaret to wonder if someone was still determined to sweep away all obstacles to the Yale Dalton scheme, the main obstacles being herself and the archduke.

As Marie fled from the affluent streets of the Upper East Side, Margaret turned her steps toward Kendall Smith's salon, which was not many blocks distant from the shoe shop.

"He's seeing no one," Kenny's guardian said. "No one at all." Her voice was melodious even through the intercom at the street level door.

"He must see me," Margaret said. "I am desperate. His party . . ." She had prepared a reason: I haven't a thing to wear to the fête.

"No." Kenny's woman was firm.

Margaret tried another tack. "And please tell him that I'm handling Archduke Niklas's business affairs now, so I need to discuss something with him."

There was momentary silence. Then a summons came down from above through the intercom.

"He has a few moments to spare." The buzzer unlocked the door, and Margaret ascended the high-priced staircase. The showroom was dark today. No flat-stomached, flat-bottomed ladies viewed the latest hot numbers in chiffon. A cloth blind covered the expanse of window that overlooked Madison Avenue. It was darkish in Kenny's workroom, except for a spotlight on a row of sketches pinned to a wall—fantastical costumes, heavy with feathers. He sat hunched up behind his desk, but when Margaret appeared he stood up, and the light glinted off his glasses.

"Don't tell me," he said gloomily. "That little experiment in ready-to-wear was a disaster. I rushed the designs, I had the wrong crowd, the wrong models, the wrong venue."

"Nonsense," Margaret said cheerfully. "They'll probably be a resounding success somewhere. Perhaps not Acapulco or Mustique, but you never know what pleases buyers in a boutique in some galleria in Indianapolis."

Kenny brightened. "Do you think so? That's a relief. What a sensible person you are, Margaret. I can trust you, and I know if you'll just agree to work with me . . . The show was Emma's doing actually. She promised great things and failed to make good, but that was Emma."

"But Kenny, she's dead. Awfully hard to keep promises under the circumstances."

He threw up his hands. "Too late now. You need advice on what to wear to my fête? Look, here's my book." He picked up an unwieldy volume with a shiny jacket. "Perfect for every fashionable woman's coffee table. Do people still have coffee tables? I know I don't. And what was it you said about the archduke?" He looked at her anxiously.

"Nothing much. I'm looking after his business affairs now." She leafed through the book. There was not much text, and that in large type so as not to weary eyes that must concentrate on the columns and columns of tiny print in *Harper's Bazaar*, *Vogue*, and *Town & Country*. The sentences were fairly simple. The illustrations were lavish. The price was very high. "It looks very good," Margaret said, and wondered how many would actually buy it, as opposed to begging for a free copy.

"The book took a *great* deal out of me," Kenny said. "I had a sweet young man who did a lot of the writing, and a perfectly marvelous girl to do the photo research. But you can't imagine the thought that had to go into it, and getting it through the press. Then there was the party to plan, and all the work to get the new line designed *and* keeping my couture clients happy. *Plus* helping everyone out with costumes for my fête."

"You're so busy," Margaret said, "that I hate to bother you about my outfit, but I was reminded that I needed something special when I was unpacking Emma's belongings from her apartment. I saw a green feather thing that I guessed you might have done for her."

"Oh that," Kenny said. "I wondered what had happened to all of her things. Yes, she was toying with idea of going as Rima the Bird Girl. I told her she wasn't quite ethereal enough, but she wouldn't listen. Do you have the costume still? Someone else might be able to use it."

"It's at my place, with all the rest of her things packed up from her apartment. There wasn't much. She'd moved most of her possessions to the archduke's apartment, where they rest even now, until he and I can decide what to do about them. He's talking of going to Palm Beach for the winter as the guest of a dear friend."

"That man." Kenny sounded exasperated. "He and Emma could be so difficult. I've never seen a man with more dear friends." He paced about, looking at Margaret from all angles. "Now what can we do to make you look fabulous? Who are you going with? Or will you be the mysterious woman alone?"

"I presume that Yale Dalton had been planning to attend with Emma, so perhaps I can substitute for her. My regular gentleman doesn't care for anything fancier than attending weddings and funerals, wearing a dark suit. Only once did he consent to wear tails, and then only to protect me from a murderer.''

"And did he?"

"In a manner of speaking," Margaret said. "He is, after all, a policeman."

"Ah. Let me think." Kenny looked at her through narrowed eyes. "Emma's bird girl wouldn't suit you, although green is a good color for you blondes. How do you feel about red? I love red personally, all shades. I loved it long before Mrs. Reagan became a photo opportunity. Remember those days?"

"I never thought red was my color," Margaret said. "It's more for the likes of Marie d'Avalon."

"She insists on going as Marie Antoinette."

"Belinda Hope is considering Marie Antoinette herself. Are we to have a room full of old queens?"

"Quite possibly," he said. "I am trying to persuade Marie to be the Firebird. Not exactly high fashion, but very glamorous." He took off his round glasses and polished them. "Gorgeous feathers, a sensational mask. I think I can convince her, and I do hope no one else thinks of it. Red really is right for her."

"Speaking of red and its various shades, that rosy creation you made for Marie which Emma borrowed was paid for by Norman Hope."

"No! Marie? And here I've been so sure that Belinda Hope had murdered Emma because of Norman." Kenny was pacing nervously. "Let me think about you some more. You wouldn't consider . . . Aha! A fan dancer. Nude body stocking and these huge fans made out of ostrich feathers. How divine!"

"I think I'd be more comfortable without an elaborate costume," Margaret said. "Perhaps merely a pretty mask with feathers from some domesticated fowl."

"Consider a hat, then," he said. "A big one with a lovely plume or two. I do have lots of old feathers. They're old enough so the bird would have been dead long since. You wouldn't be endangering anything if that concerns you. A dress with leg-o-mutton sleeves and a hint of a bustle. Very Gibson Girlish. No? Where did my powers of persuasion go?''

''You're very persuasive, Kenny, but I believe I'll stick with my favorite gown that I've not had much occasion to wear, and a mask. It's purple satin.

''Then I'll have a lovely mask made up with purple feathers and a touch of glitter. I'll phone you when it's ready. I do wish I had Emma's little costume. Well, never mind. I can redo it in a minute.''

''I've taken up too much of your time,'' Margaret said. ''I have to go around to see Yale about business.''

''Do put in a good word for me with Yale. Just in case he's wavering about . . . well, the business I have with him.''

''You have an impressive business plan,'' Margaret said.

''You've seen it?'' Kenny was surprised.

''No, not exactly.'' Margaret kicked herself mentally for not remembering that the business plan was among the confidential papers Emma had stolen. ''It must have been Dalton or Marie who mentioned it. Or perhaps Emma.''

''I see,'' Kenny said. ''Always Emma. The source of so much trouble, and not a deep thought or the slightest understanding in that empty little head—cut down in her prime, but there was a hard heart in that rosy bosom rising above that rosy dress. She'll haunt us forever.'' He shook his head. ''Does Calvin Klein have to put up with this kind of nonsense?''

Chapter 18

"*I*'ve been wantin' to have a talk with you," Yale Dalton said. "Me and Tina and Wayne were thinkin' it was time to straighten some things out. How's about this evening?"

Margaret fidgeted in the pay phone from which she was calling Yale. "I was hoping we could meet now."

"I'm afraid that's not possible," Yale said. "I got a meeting here in just a few minutes with your friend the prince."

"Paul? Whatever for?"

"Oh, a little investment maybe. He seems to think we got a good program here that'll turn those Italian things, leeray, into big big bucks."

"He's definitely investing?" Margaret had a panicked moment thinking of Paul selling the Ferrari and investing the proceeds in Dalton's scheme.

"We sure do hope so." Dalton chuckled. "I'd hate to think he's coming 'round just cause he's sweet on our Tina."

"Shall I come around seven then?" Margaret said quickly.

"Sounds good," Yale said. "See you then."

Margaret frantically sought out another quarter and dialed Paul's number at the bank. He had left only moments before. She flagged a cab and held her breath as it careened around corners and finally left her alive but shaken on a corner near the Villa d'Este Hotel.

Paul had chosen to arrive by cab, rather than by Ferrari—

unless, as Margaret feared, the Ferrari was no longer his to arrive in. Margaret caught him at the entrance to the hotel.

"Whatever you're planning to do, don't," she said, out of breath from her perilous dash across the street through traffic.

"Margaret! What is it that I am supposed to be going to do?"

"Invest your ill-gotten gains in castles built on sand. Literally."

"I have no gains, ill or good. You know that. What I am engaged in is trying to determine what the delicious Tina is up to. She is charming, and then she is cold. She lures me to her, and puts me aside. I have been playing these games all my life, and I would like to win one of them. The promise of investment makes me welcome."

"Do be careful of Tina, Paul. I fear that her affections are committed elsewhere. Besides, I can't get it out of my mind that Emma could have been murdered by a woman."

"I do not believe that a woman who attracts me so greatly is capable of murder," Paul said, "although I do believe her capable of other doubtful behavior." Then he frowned. "Why a woman?"

"Emma was dressed for the party when Marcus came to the door to deliver the food, but she was not dressed when she was found."

"The murderer might have removed the dress. I myself have had occasion . . . That is to say, it is not difficult to persuade a woman to . . ."

"But she was wearing an old robe, and even in undress Emma would have wanted to look good for a man. On the other hand, I can imagine she might not care about a woman seeing her less than glamorous. Then I can see Marie becoming furious about the gown, or Belinda about Norman. Or Tina might have decided to speed up the progress of their business scheme, and deal directly with the archduke by eliminating Emma."

"Well, then," Paul said. "Which one was it?"

Margaret hesitated. "Now that you ask the question, I

believe I know," she said slowly. "I should have thought of it before."

"Speak," Paul said.

"No, I can't tell you yet. I have to think it through. Now run along and see the Dalton crowd, and don't do anything foolish."

"I am afraid that will always be the case with me," Paul said, "but at least foolish is better than truly stupid."

"I'll wait for you if you aren't to be long."

"Not long, I think," Paul said. "I will look into Tina's eyes, as she is surrounded by her colleagues, and I shall know. It will take only a little time then for them to discover that I will not invest because there is nothing to invest."

"No, don't say that yet. Tell them you will not invest now because you have heard rumors. Mention a name or two. Charles Stark. Some bankers you know. See how they react. It will have some bearing on how I deal with the archduke's affairs. I will definitely be waiting. Meet me at the Plaza in an hour? The Palm Court. I have to make a phone call or two."

Margaret beat out a businessman to a corner phone booth and rang Kasparian.

"Niklas was here for a time, looking at the Persian miniatures. The ones I like so much they're never for sale. He's gone out."

"Where did he go?" Margaret asked. "I feel this is not a safe city until everyone is convinced that he has handed over all decisions to me. Is he coming back?"

"I do not pry into a distinguished gentleman's activities. He did mention a gift. Perhaps he was thinking of acquiring some token to repay your kindness."

"He has very little money," Margaret said.

"Wrong. He has quite a bit. Remember that he did a very fine job of selling some overvalued but beautiful pieces to Mrs. Courtney. He might have also been about some other business," Kasparian said. "I did not enquire."

There was no answer to a call to her own apartment. The archduke was still loose in the city.

While Margaret retired to the Plaza Hotel to enjoy the rejuvenated Palm Court—did she recognize the rejuvenator herself?—the players in the life and death of Emma, Lady Ross, struggled with their own concerns.

Marie d'Avalon came safely home, clutching her rhinestone comb and cursing Margaret for causing her to abandon the exquisite alligator pumps that were so superbly comfortable. She punched out a number on her telephone.

"I was with that horrendous woman this afternoon. She will ruin our plans. Life was much simpler when I was a happy young woman enjoying pleasures when they arose."

The person she was speaking to seemingly reminded her that it had been some time since she was either happy or young.

"What a wretched thing to say! I am always good-humored. But if she discovers who murdered that silly cow, she will not hesitate to report it to the authorities, and I tell you, she is looking and thinking. I can tell by what she says."

There was a longish pause.

"Of course I did not murder Emma. You are much more likely." She slammed down the receiver.

To calm her agitation, Marie unpacked her ingredients for cosmetics, and was determined to discover a really interesting combination of essences and colors to wipe away the encroaching years. She did not understand why people were so concerned about Emma Ross. She was both a competitor and an obstacle to everyone, and Marie had no patience with either.

There was friction as usual in the Hope household.

"I know you saw her last evening," Belinda said. "One stuck-up Brit is gone, and one even more impossible takes her place. Do you have some deep yen for foreign women?"

"Lady Margaret is involved in handling the same business as Emma was, vis-à-vis the archduke," Norman said quietly. Now that he had seemingly come to the very end of his personal and professional rope, he felt calm.

"Nevertheless, you were seen huddling over your frosty drinks, head to head, nose to nose. And she was here yesterday, you know, sooo polite and suggesting all manner of brazen things. Well, I know how to take care of women like her and that other trollop. Except—'' Belinda almost giggled ''—the other trollop was forced to retire from trolloping, wasn't she?''

"Please do be careful what you say, Belinda," Norman said. "It could get you into trouble if someone thought that 'taking care' of Emma implied murder."

"What nonsense," Belinda said, and swept away to be cross once more at the decorator who had punished her with art deco in her boudoir.

Not a happy marriage, Norman thought. Perhaps she'll settle for the apartment if the other business falls through.

The maid, who was rather ugly and very efficient—both features to commend her to Belinda—summoned him to a telephone call on his private line.

"Who is it?" Belinda demanded from her doorway.

"The party did not give a name," the maid said. "It was difficult to hear."

Did Norman see just the hint of a wink as he passed the maid? It was comforting to know that someone in the household appeared to be on his side, although that did not bode well for her continued employment.

"I have told you a hundred times that you *must* ask the name. Was it a man or a woman?" Belinda was on the crest of her fury.

"I could not determine, madame," the maid said. "The voice was strangled, as though the throat was being grasped by powerful hands." The maid marched away to her quarters.

"I am being sabotaged by the help," Belinda said to no one. "I will never again hire an aspiring novelist to work for me."

Norman took the phone, which had no other extensions in the entire apartment. "Norman Hope here."

"I wish to tell you not to speak to the Priam woman. She is a terrrrible woman."

"Marie, I have asked you not to call me at home."

"But it is an emergency. She is not to be trusted."

"I know that," Norman said. "Thank you for calling. I have to go now."

"I *do* have to go now," Kenny Smith said into his special order silver and gray super Trimline phone. "There's nothing you can tell me that I didn't hear eons ago. And listen, my precious, I promise you that everything is going to be fine. We'll all be very rich in the end, trust Kenny."

He hung up, and to calm himself he took up an advance copy of *Feathers and Fashion* and leafed through it to admire the tasteful blocks of text and the stunning pictures. It was so big, so beautiful, and so expensive. He would have to sell fifteen thousand copies to begin to make back the money he'd spent on having it produced. The party would help, and if he could persuade the bookers for the "Today Show" that he was a delightful antidote to bad economic news, drugs, and major plane crashes, he'd be set. Then there was Carson and the daytime talk shows. And print media: *New York*, *People*, and the big fashion magazines. When the boutiques got rolling, he could do personal appearances to thrill his public. There were only one or two difficult but not insurmountable problems in his way. In any case, he thought he could handle Lady Margaret Priam before she did any damage.

Yale Dalton, Wayne D. Wayne, and Tina Corrado sat in a semicircle of armchairs in their suite at the Villa d'Este.

"So he's not going to invest jes' now," Wayne said. "Rumors about the city. What the hell is that boy talkin' about? What do we know about him anyhow? Anybody ever ask Marie about him?"

Tina picked the phone and dialed. "Marie, do you know anything about a Prince Paul Castrocani? Italian. I've been out with him, but . . ." Tina frowned and Yale and Wayne leaned forward as though to draw Marie's words from the receiver. Then Tina hung up. "Marie knows the name. He's been around the city for a while. She says his mother is supposed to be the second or third richest woman in Texas.

Isn't that a surprise? The beautiful blonde Mrs. Benton Hoopes.''

"Texas? You got your dumb blondes in every state, but Texas got more than its share," Wayne said. He poured himself a stiff bourbon and ignored Tina's baleful look. "As long as there's money behind him, don't matter much."

The blonde in question answered a call from Margaret on her car phone somewhere in North Dallas.

Carolyn Sue Hoopes said, "You say these folks talked first about leasing oil equipment, and then building a city in the desert without an airport, and *then* helping that tart Marie d'Avalon start a health spa? Sounds like if they drilled for oil in their brains they'd come up dry. And that little Kenny Smith is mixed up in this too? I bought a couple of things from him once, but he started using synthetic fabrics. When a man lets his moral values slip like that, I don't want anythin' more to do with him. Is my precious boy involved with these felons?"

"Not really, Carolyn Sue. He's been doing a bit of detective work for me."

"Margaret, I love that boy, I loved his daddy, even though there was no living with him. I want to see Paul make something of himself, and so does his stepdaddy. Ben Hoopes is as fine a man as you'll find anywhere. Not the same as Aldo, of course. He was a lot of fun. The places we used to go, the people we'd meet. I even sometimes miss the old Castrocani villa with the plaster fallin' down and those faded old frescos all over the place. I used to get the willies sometimes having a bunch of saints staring down at me when I was havin' my dinner. My, will you listen to me talkin' about the past? You think I'm gettin' old?"

"You? Never."

"I do say money is the one thing that can stop the clock," Carolyn Sue Dennis Castrocani Hoopes said. "Run those names by me again."

"Yale Dalton, Wayne D. Wayne, and Tina Corrado."

"Nope. Never heard of a one of them. And I know just

about everyone that has anything to do with oil in the entire Southwest. That's their real names?''

"To tell the truth, I have no idea."

"I've seen a pile of con men in my time," Carolyn Sue said. "They like to change their names to keep the law off their tails. Now you hold on a minute. There's a call on the other line."

Margaret did not know many people with two car phones, and she was impressed.

Carolyn Sue returned. "That was Ben wanting to know if I needed the jet the next couple of days. He's off to California. I tell you, Margaret, it's not easy keeping track of a busy man. Aldo was much simpler. He'd sit in a café for hours and just look at the girls. You sure you're taking good care of my boy?"

"I am taking care," Margaret said, "but the Ferrari is controlling him."

"Good-lookin' car, isn't it? I just couldn't resist it."

"Neither can he," Margaret said. "Come to visit in New York soon."

"As long as you can promise me you're still seein' Sam De Vere," Carolyn Sue said. "I wish you two would decide to get married or something permanent."

"I think what we have is fairly permanent," Margaret said. "Unless, of course, he catches me looking for a murderer again."

Margaret left the public phone at the Plaza and returned to her table in the Palm Court to wait for Carolyn Sue's "boy."

"They seemed nervous today," Paul said when he joined her. "Perhaps Emma's murder and their association with her have turned back the tide of eager investors."

"I didn't suppose they would confide in you about this scam," Margaret said.

"No, but I observed the shortness of temper my Texas grandfather used to display when his dubious deals were not proceeding well. I have often wondered how he managed to stay out of jail."

"I spoke to your mother just now," Margaret said. "She had never heard of Dalton or Wayne."

"She did not suggest that I return the Ferrari, did she?" Paul asked.

"You are still safe in that," Margaret said. "She seemed rather proud of herself for having thought to give it to you. I am seeing Yale at seven. I want to be certain I have an escort for Kenny's *Feathers and Fashion* thing. And you are going too."

"I am?"

"I thought you would escort Tina. I can fix that. We can set Wayne D. Wayne up with Marie, and I will go with Yale. Although I am fairly certain who murdered Emma, there's still the archduke's land to negotiate about—and I shouldn't like to put a stop to everyone's unseemly desire to make fools of themselves in fancy dress."

Chapter 19

"*Mr. Dalton's* suite does not answer," the operator at the Villa d'Este said. "Would you care to leave a message with our message center?"

"Not just now, thank you." Margaret felt she was losing all the suspects. Three missing from the Dalton crowd, no one at home at the Hope apartment except for a maid who didn't know where they were, and the phone at Marie's apartment rang and rang. Kenny had left his showroom some time before according to his guardian, saying he was off to the health club to exercise and then walk his puppies.

"Puppies?"

"He has a dalmation puppy he calls Athena and a handsome old mongrel named Richie. They take walks and lie around and watch trash TV. If you call his answering service, you can leave him a message."

"Not important," Margaret said. "I'll ring him tomorrow at the showroom."

The archduke was also still among the missing. Margaret bravely called the number Kasparian had told her was to be used only in case of emergency, such as the discovery of a long-lost trove of treasures looted from the sack of the Forbidden City.

"I ought to have told you," Kasparian said. "Niklas said something about consulting a lawyer on personal business, and perhaps seeing his physician, as he complained of tiredness. Then he spoke of finding Mrs. Courtney's knightly decoration, to cement her invitation for Palm Beach. He asked me not to speak of his plans, so I did not."

"He should have told me."

"My dear Margaret, I should think as a woman who is acquainted with persons of very high status, you would understand that people like Niklas do not feel they have to answer to anyone, even the earl's sister, if they choose not to. He is, I believe, more or less authentic. Last of his line, which might not have been very important on the stage of history, but genuine. I would have to look it up."

Margaret had a sudden vision of Niklas, last of his line, beset by muggers and vagrants as he tottered through Times Square, confused by traffic and seeking a way uptown to his old apartment to rummage about for Mrs. Courtney's decoration.

"I ought to try to locate him," Margaret said. "Sorry to have disturbed you at home."

"I understand your concern," Kasparian said. "He has a gift for involving kind strangers in his life, who then become dear friends willing to take care of him. Remarkable man, don't you think?"

"Rather," Margaret said.

"So is young Marcus. He does not care for the Persian miniatures, but he is quite taken with fu dogs and the temple guardians on display in the shop."

"Don't put too many breakables in his way," Margaret said. "I don't know that he's fully aware of the value of some of your things. But then, I'm not sure even someone like Mrs. Courtney understands their true value beyond the sums you charge."

Again no one answered at Yale Dalton's suite, so Margaret left a message cancelling her seven o'clock appointment and set off uptown to the archduke's Riverside Drive apartment. Traffic did not cooperate, but it was a truth that Manhattan traffic seldom did cooperate, except around six o'clock on a Sunday morning. This day it seemed to take hours to move across town and then north some fifty blocks. By the time she reached the archduke's building, she was rather cross that he did not choose to spend money on a telephone.

She rang the doorbell under the ducal coronet, but there was no response. Now she was crosser because she had made the trip in vain. He might have been invited to dine by his new friend Mrs. Courtney, or another dear friend, for surely Archduke Niklas had acquaintances in the city other than Emma and herself. She went outside and peered into the low, street-level window that looked in on the kitchen. She would have been relieved to see him deaf to the doorbell, puttering about making his own tea, but there was no one to be seen. She looked up and tried to determine if there was light behind the tall curtained windows of the big cluttered room on the first floor. It was impossible to tell. The other street level window, which she remembered as high on the wall of his sitting room, also had drawn curtains, but here she thought she detected a thin line of light where the curtain met the bottom of the window.

Back in the foyer, she did not hesitate to ring the bell of an apartment on the floor above the lobby, with three names handwritten on a strip of cardboard taped under the button. A male voice asked who it was, and Margaret put on her best upper-class British accent.

"Lady Margaret Priam," she said. "I am worried about the old gentleman on the ground floor. I can't get him to answer." She was buzzed in, and a plump, balding, and earnest academic peered down at her over the banister.

"You can usually get in just by leaning on the door," he said. "Is something wrong, do you think? Nice old fellow, very courtly. Called himself a duke."

"I'm not sure," Margaret said. "There's a light on, but no answer to my ring."

"Do you have a key?"

"Yes. He gave me one to the apartment." She turned the knob of the archduke's door. "In any case, it seems to be open. He's rather forgetful. Thanks awfully for letting me in." The academic had already retreated to his ivory tower.

The big room was in darkness, and she ran her hand along the wall beside the door in the hope of finding a light switch.

The room did not blaze into light, but the wall sconces switched on and shed a faint glow. It seemed that the archduke might have been rummaging about, for there were open drawers and open cartons. She froze at a faint scrabbling noise in the passageway that led from the back stairs to the kitchen. Then there was silence. Mice in the cupboards, perhaps.

"Hullo? It's Margaret," she called from the top of the main stairs that led down to the archduke's private rooms. There was no answer from below. She started cautiously down the stairs into the darkness. She felt her way along the hall to the sitting room, where there was a faint line of light at the bottom of the closed door. She was relieved to think the archduke was dozing after a busy day to gather strength to return to Margaret's apartment. As she pushed open the door, she started at the sound of the door above slamming shut. She could not remember if she had shut the front door firmly behind her. But there was silence, and the moment of anxiety passed.

Archduke Niklas was sitting in his chair, his old distinguished head nodding and his eyes closed. A box of medals had fallen from his lap to the floor, spilling its contents: enameled Maltese crosses on moire ribbons of red and blue and white, intricately worked chains from which dangled starbursts in gold and silver, a slim gem-encrusted dagger, a ring with a huge square-cut green stone in a heavy gold setting. One of the archduke's hands loosely held a silver medallion on a purple ribbon.

"It's time to go, sir," Margaret said gently.

He did not move in the midst of his dreams of the grandeur that had vanished, and the games of survival he had played through the decades, and his young man's frolics with the likes of Paul Castrocani's grandfather. Perhaps he dreamt of the warm place to the south where he would spend the winter, and the other warm places where he had gambled at baccarat and gazed passionately at rich young ladies who were so eager to return the favor with gifts; that cursed, useless land that was more of a burden than an asset.

She reached out and touched his hand. It was cold. She

leaned toward him, to be reassured by the rise and fall of his breathing. She detected nothing, and then she surrendered to the reality she had been trying to deny. Archduke Niklas was no longer alive. It seemed that he had simply gone to sleep in his regal armchair and passed quietly into his new kingdom. Sudden sharp tears blurred her sight for a moment. The last of his line.

Then Margaret roused herself and looked about carefully. Suspicious though she was of all the connivers after his land, or rather the idea of his land, there was no clear indication that he had died unnaturally. She saw no sign of a struggle, no cup to hold a drink laced with poison, no blood, no bruise to show a killing blow. She looked for a long moment at a square pillow covered with an old petit point cover. She lifted it. It was soft, filled with goose down. Someone might have crept in and used it to smother the shallow breath of an old man already asleep. She squeezed the pillow again and dropped it where she had found it. Then she picked up the medallion: Mrs. Courtney's Order of the Silver Crane. A long-legged bird with outstretched wings was engraved upon it. She slipped it into her pocket to be delivered one day to Mrs. Courtney, the archduke's last great friend. She thought for a moment and decided to take the big ring, which was possibly an emerald, and possibly too valuable to leave lying about.

On the floor beside the archduke's chair was a long brown envelope with her name written upon it in a spidery, ornate hand. She put it into her handbag and ascended the stairs to find the academic resident on the floor above and his telephone.

"What a shame," the archduke's neighbor said. "He was very old, though. A relative of yours?" The academic's desk was piled with books, and the telephone buried beneath a clutter of scholarly journals. The apartment was awash with the sound of a Schubert string quartet.

"No," Margaret said. "Just a dear friend."

It took some time to locate De Vere and wait for him and an ambulance and the various persons who were required to clear up the death of Archduke Niklas.

"In spite of Lady Ross's murder," De Vere said, "I don't think this is anything other than death by old age. We'll look into it. Are you all right?"

"I'm very sad," Margaret said. "He had a number of things to look forward to." The envelope in her bag begged to be opened, but she could not do that in De Vere's presence.

When matters had been settled at the archduke's apartment, De Vere took her arm and led her out into the night.

"You haven't been seeking a murderer, have you? I know I haven't been around much to keep you in line. . . ."

"I have been thinking about Emma," Margaret said. "I couldn't avoid it, could I? The archduke has been staying with me for the past few days. And I've had no indication that the police are any closer to finding out who murdered her."

"They have certain suspicions. Do you know Norman Hope?"

"Indeed I do," Margaret said. "But surely it was not Norman."

"You sound so certain. You *have* been poking around in matters that shouldn't concern you." De Vere was stern. "The financial aspects of Norman Hope's life do not hold up to close scrutiny. And there is his former relationship with the lady. Russo is looking at him closely. There is as yet little evidence, however, and judges and juries and district attorneys do like hard evidence. Who have you come up with as the likely suspect?"

"No one at all," Margaret said hastily, and hated to lie to De Vere. She was absolutely certain who had killed Emma, and had no way at all of proving it. "Since you have to return to your work," she said, "could you drop me at Poppy Dill's place? She'd never forgive me if I did not give her a firsthand account of the passing of the archduke."

"It's *never* too late for news," Poppy said, when Margaret informed her of her reason for visiting at such a late hour. "You're sure there was no indication of foul play?"

"None," Margaret said, and did not even mention the little pillow.

"Stress," Poppy said wisely. "The loss of his little girlfriend in such a terrible way."

" 'Old age,' the doctor said." Margaret remembered the slamming door. "A peaceful death in old age."

"That's the way I'd like to go," Poppy said, and left unspoken the implication that she was not the sort to die, ever. She settled Margaret into a comfortable chair in her boudoir and patted her hand. "Don't be upset, dear. My, but isn't it interesting that that ancient man still had the power to enthrall a young woman like yourself."

"He was quite endearing," Margaret said. "I wish I might have known him better, especially now when it seems that he might have been all he claimed to be."

"Really?" Poppy was suddenly alert. "I had no idea. I shall have an exclusive tribute in the column. 'Modest, unsung, the last of a great line has died peacefully in our city, taking with him the secrets of history. . . .' "

"It wasn't such a great line, Poppy. Only some dreary little duchy off in the wilds of Europe. Niklas inflated the titles and the territories."

"I don't care," Poppy said, "and neither will my readers." She flexed her fingers, eager to get to her typewriter. "I must have a file on him someplace, although I know him mostly by reputation." Poppy's locked files of the history of the social world were legendary.

"At least now that he is gone, the desperate pursuit of his land will end, and all that is left for me to do is to find a way to prove who the murderer of Emma is."

Now Poppy was really interested. "You know?"

"I believe so. I wonder if the archduke didn't have an idea as well."

"And that person contrived some way to make his death look natural before the archduke told the authorities." Poppy was thrilled. "And you're here to tell me this, so that if anything happens to you . . ." She waited expectantly for Margaret to reveal the name.

"I'm staying with a natural death for the archduke. And

as for Emma, I'm not ready to share my suspicions. I'm here only to have you stand by while I open this.'' Margaret took from her bag the envelope left her by the archduke. ''It was beside his chair.''

''And you haven't opened it yet? I couldn't have waited a second.'' Poppy watched as Margaret slit the envelope open. ''Does he reveal the murderer? No, wait—his numbered Swiss bank account.''

Margaret shook her head as she read. ''Neither of those things,'' she said. ''He seems to have rewritten his will, in my favor. Listen to his letter to me: 'I had hoped to provide Emma with some security when I was gone, for the sake of her kindness to me, but she died first, and there is no one left now except you. I make you the heir of my possessions, with the hope that by the time you read this, we will have been friends for many years.' '' Margaret dropped the letter into her lap and sighed deeply.

''What a *divine* story!'' Poppy said. ''How romantic! And what do you suppose you have inherited?''

''A few bits of gold and ribbon, an emerald ring that might be worth quite a bit, a few letters written by famous dead people—and that damned land. It's going to haunt me forever.''

''Unless you unload it,'' Poppy said. ''Let's be practical. People want it, so you might as well sell it to them. Raise the price.''

''Poppy, I can't honestly allow that crowd to bilk the ignorant public by having them invest in a city made of smoke and little else.''

''Margaret,'' Poppy said sternly, ''the people who will invest are not ignorant. They are greedy. They may be dreamers, but they are greedy dreamers, and if they have enough money to give it to the likes of Norman Hope, they deserve to lose it. Besides,'' she added, ''they have probably all done something much more wicked than Norman and his friends are contemplating.''

''You don't convince me,'' Margaret said. ''However, I shall hold out the land as an enticement until I have rounded up Emma's killer. Then . . .'' She paused.

"*Don't* be coy," Poppy begged. "I must know."

Margaret said, "I'll sell it to the people who really want it for what it is, a patch of desert."

"How boring," Poppy said. "I understood there was to be a grand spa."

"Who told you that?"

"Marie d'Avalon, of course. She promised me its use free for a lifetime."

"And Kenny Smith promises you free clothes. The Hopes give you the use of the big white limousine which is only borrowed from the actual owner." Margaret was exasperated, but amused.

"Well, there's nothing wrong with that," Poppy said complacently. "I only need a car once or twice a year. And if it's a funeral, you *know* I always try to find a black limo."

"Poppy, you're a real pleasure to know. I'll have to see that Mrs. Phillip Courtney receives the decoration the archduke intended to bestow on her, and perhaps you can write about that too."

"He knew Genevieve that well? He was amazing. I can't wait to write it up."

"Hold off for a few days, would you? The story could get better, and then you'd have a real exclusive."

"You mean the murderer? Well . . ." Poppy hesitated. "All right, but it must be an *absolute* exclusive. When?"

"Oh, perhaps by the time the *Feathers and Fashion* party has come and gone. Concentrate on writing about that."

Poppy sniffed. "It's not top drawer. I've only mentioned it because of the clothes and the limo."

"I understand Dianne and Charlie Stark and a lot of their people are going."

"Really? Why?"

"Apparently even adults like to play dress up," Margaret said.

Chapter 20

Margaret planned to say the same thing to everyone: "Yes, the dear archduke is gone. Yes, he left everything to me, but you understand it was not much. Such a sweet gesture. No, I have no idea what I'll do with the land he supposedly owned, but there's a deed about somewhere."

She seldom had the opportunity to make the entire statement. The people concerned were more interested in making clear their own positions. It was surprising how quickly news of the Archduke Niklas's demise had spread, in spite of Poppy's promise not to elaborate on the details in her "Social Scene" column.

Belinda Hope was first on the phone, even while Margaret was attempting to arrange the matter of the final disposition of the archduke himself, which was not an inexpensive matter. It was to be hoped that the sale of the dynastic emerald—quite fine, it turned out—would eventually cover the costs incurred.

"This isn't going to screw up my party—Kenny's party—is it? I mean, Emma's murder was one thing, and it was bad enough to be there when that woman found the body, but another murder connected to her would be just too much. It wasn't murder, tell me it wasn't." Belinda was bordering on hysteria.

"As far as I know it wasn't," Margaret said. "In any case,

the archduke wasn't to be a featured player at your fête, was he?''

"Of course not! I suppose if Emma were alive, she might have brought him along, although I didn't specifically encourage it. If he had had the price of a ticket—very low, barely more than two people would spend on an average dinner out, just a couple of hundred dollars. That's the way Kenny wanted it. The people who got personal invitations from Kenny don't have to pay anything at all. But even they will think twice about coming if there's a murderer on the loose.''

"Belinda, please calm down. It was merely an unexpected but entirely logical death from old age.''

"But what is it going to mean for Norman's business? I had plans. That is, I . . . we were counting on having the project he was working on, the development, the land. . . .''

"I haven't decided,'' Margaret said. "Have the police been around to see Norman again?''

"No! Do you mean to our apartment? I couldn't look the doorman in the eye. Norman would have told me if they were bothering him at the office. Surely they don't think . . .''

"It is only that I heard from highly placed sources that the police were rethinking suspects,'' Margaret said. "It's probably nothing, although since Norman was Emma's financial advisor . . .''

"*Not* for ages. I told you that was all over long ago.''

"I suppose they'll get around to you again, too.''

"Me? *Me?* They'd be better off questioning those villains who started all this. There's no predicting the kind of duplicity Yale Dalton practices. He's . . . He's . . .''

Margaret mentally supplied the missing word. A cad. A deceiver. A man without morals. Probably rather like many men Belinda knew.

"He's agreed to escort me to the *Feathers and Fashion* party,'' Margaret said. "For business reasons. I'll certainly have to discuss my thoughts on the archduke's land with Norman one day soon. The archduke's death has changed things.''

Now Margaret had to make certain that Yale Dalton did

escort her. She was summoned to meet the trio in the Villa d'Este's intimate dark bar, with thick carpets and subdued music, and very good crystal for the drinks.

"I'm really sorry I got all mixed up the other day about when we were to be meetin'," Yale said. "And then to hear about the old fella dyin' jes' like that. Makes you think. Nobody's safe."

"Safe?" Margaret said. She was facing the three of them across a table. "Do you mean nobody's 'safe' because we all might be murdered in our beds?"

Wayne D. Wayne seemed to gurgle and grunt, and then caught himself.

"He died so peacefully," Margaret said. "It was touching. I suppose you've heard that he managed to see a lawyer about changing his will. He left everything to me, and then he was gone, the dear, dear man." Margaret hoped she was not overdoing grief and sentimentality. "I do regret, Mr. Wayne, that the archduke did not have the opportunity to grant you the title you desired. It was much on his mind. . . ."

"Well, now," Wayne said. "If it's a matter of a little, oh let's call it expense money to help you along, you being the one who inherited . . ."

"Alas," she said, "the inheritance of his earthly possessions does not include his dynastic rights. I am afraid I am unable to confer titles or knightly orders"—she smiled prettily—"even though a lady. However, I do know of people who do that sort of thing. Do not give up hope, Mr. Wayne."

"It was jes' an idea," Wayne mumbled. Margaret thought she heard the hitherto silent Tina mutter something like "Stupid old fool."

"About that land," Dalton said, and at last Margaret had a chance to repeat her rehearsed speech.

"Yes, he left everything to me, such a sweet gesture. I have no idea yet what I'll want to do about the land."

"It's only good for a major development," Dalton said.

"I've seen the plans," Margaret said, "and I know what it's good for."

"We'd be glad to come to some fair solution," Tina said.

She was drumming her fingers on the table. "The archduke was willing to let us purchase it for a reasonable sum. It was Emma who got greedy."

"Ah, greed," Margaret said. "Not an uncommon reason for murder. Well, it is too soon for me to decide. He was such an old friend of my family's. He knew my father the earl in the old days." She decided not to fabricate a story of how the archduke used to bounce her on his knee as an infant. "What I do want to have cleared up is who murdered Emma. Naturally, I have my own ideas." She left it at that.

"We didn't know him well," Dalton said. "Emma kinda introduced us."

"So I understood," Margaret said. "And if Emma was murdered because of a big piece of land nobody's ever seen, I suppose I should worry about me being next."

"I hope you ain't accusing us," Wayne began, and stopped. Evidently Yale or Tina had managed a hefty kick under the table.

"What an idea! Naturally, I shall take precautions until the police resolve the situation. And I will find time very soon, Yale, to sit down and talk about your plans. First, however, I have a big, big favor to ask."

"Whatever you want, little lady," Yale said.

She leaned across the table. "Could I *beg* you to escort me to Kendall Smith's fancy dress party? It would make me feel so safe, and I promise I won't be wearing anything outlandish. We could all attend together! Tina and dear Prince Paul. Mr. Wayne and Marie. That would be such fun!"

So eager were they to remain in the good graces of the one who controlled the land, they all nodded vigorous assent without even thinking.

"I do feel sorry for Marie," Margaret said. "There was some relationship between her family and the archduke, and I believe she had some expectations. I hope she's not terribly upset."

"Well, she is," Wayne said. There was apparently another silencing kick on the table. "She was right fond of him. Like a daddy to her, he was."

"Poor Marie. I still have to go through the archduke's

apartment and pack up his things. Perhaps there's some little token Marie might cherish.'' Margaret was under no illusions that Marie d'Avalon would cherish anything of the archduke's, unless it were everything. "And I must look about for the deed to the land. He has piles of old papers, and I'm sure it's tucked away somewhere.''

Not long after, Margaret had the opportunity to offer some little token to Marie herself.

"I rang you to find out about the plans for my spa. I do not want any of the archduke's rrrrrubbish. What will you do about the land? This is verrrry important to me. The women of America—the right sort of women—need my beauty secrets. I have a mission. Even you who is no longer verrry young must understand what I offer. Did you say you do not yet have the deed?''

"I said it,'' Margaret said, "but not, I think, to you. In any case, I shall make no decision until we learn who murdered Emma.''

"I have forgotten that she was ever alive, let alone that she is dead.'' Margaret was by now accustomed to Marie ending a telephone call by slamming down the receiver.

Margaret did not have much time to mull over Marie's call, because the next call was from Kenny Smith.

"I am quite tired,'' Margaret said, "so please don't ask me about the archduke and the land and what's to become of the backing for your line of clothes.''

"You poor darling, *what* a time you have had. Marie said you were highly distressed.''

"I might have thought it was Marie who was distressed,'' Margaret said.

"I trust my chums to do what's right,'' Kenny said. "The line and the boutiques are going to practically mint money, you know. All it takes is the right backing.'' Margaret knew enough to understand that the most eligible backer was Yale Dalton, provided he could proceed with accumulating money from innocent investors who saw dollar signs under a cactus. "I called to tell you that your mask is ready, and it's divine. As long as you keep your promise to wear purple.''

"I promise," she said. "I'll fetch it in a day or two. I have to go around to the archduke's place tomorrow afternoon to pack things up. Lots of papers to go through, the deed to find . . ."

"Perhaps there's a deed to a castle as well as to that land," Kenny said.

"Perhaps," Margaret said. "It's hard to know anything for certain. Except that I do know, I think, who murdered Emma."

"Not really! I didn't imagine anyone would ever find out. I do have to run," he said. "Simply everyone has suddenly realized that only *I* can whip up just the kind of understated and perfect masquerade dress to set them apart."

"Apart?"

"Apart from Marie Antoinette, darling." Then Kenny was gone to his bolts of fabric and bales of feathers.

Paul did not sound happy when he called. "I am advised by the delectable Tina that I am to accompany her to a party where I am to be dressed in feathers. I do not think I can do this."

"I suggest you wear tails," Margaret said, "and claim to be a penguin. You look perfectly wonderful undisguised, so there is no reason to believe that a costume will improve you."

"I am relieved," Paul said. "I spoke to my mother today. She does not approve of me being drawn into a murder. Nor does De Vere."

"You haven't told De Vere anything," Margaret said.

"On the contrary," Paul said. "He told me. He is holding his temper. And you do understand, I hope, that he continues to care deeply about you."

"I know," Margaret said. "What am I to do?"

"I am incapable of suggesting marriage," Paul said, "since I do not advise people to do what I will not do."

"You would marry if she were rich enough," Margaret said.

"Yes," he said slowly, "but I do believe that love is very important. I should like to love a rich woman."

Chapter 21

M̲argaret went around to Kasparian's shop to borrow Marcus.

"I'm going up to the archduke's apartment this afternoon to clear it out," she told Kasparian. "It was only his to use during his lifetime, and the managing company wants everything out. Marcus will be useful to move out boxes to my car. The furniture is being given away to charity. Marcus has met your satisfaction, I hope?"

"He comes to work more frequently than you do," Kasparian said, "but I do understand the pressures of solving a murder without the aid of the authorities. I'm glad the old man wasn't also murdered."

"He might have been, you know. But I doubt if anyone could prove it. It would have been the same person who murdered Emma, so I believe I will let the archduke rest in peace and concentrate on the other murder."

Kasparian shook his round bald head. "Terrible things go on in this city. And yes, Marcus is satisfactory for the moment. The other boy I had was so lacking in dexterity that I was constantly in suspense about which precious piece would be irreparably damaged."

"Marcus," Margaret said, "I would hope that you could pick up my mask from Kendall Smith's salon just a couple of blocks up on Madison. I don't want to risk getting involved in a long conversation about his fête. Then meet me uptown at the archduke's apartment. I'll take my car to carry away odds and ends." Margaret seldom used the car she garaged expensively in the basement of her apartment building. Now and then in summer she did like to drive the length of Long Island to Montauk at the very end, bypassing the crowded streets and unimaginably expensive real estate of the Hamptons where once farmers toiled in their potato fields. "I'm afraid my vehicle isn't as glamorous as Prince Paul's."

"Guy could get killed owning a car like that," Marcus said. "I could meet you whenever you say. I can carry the heavy stuff."

"There won't be much," she said. Margaret had spent a good deal of time in intimate company with old and rare furniture at home at Priam's Priory. She knew that the archduke's furniture was merely old and ordinary, suitable only for resale at bargain rates at the thrift shop of the charitable organization that was sending a truck. She had promised a bookcase to the helpful academic on the floor above, for which he was grateful, but since his field was philosophy, he rejected the possibility of acquiring the archduke's library of biographies of Prussian generals and memoirs of discarded mistresses of minor royalty.

The big old building was quiet. The graduate students were off at their scholarly pursuits in libraries and lectures. The flashlight she had brought with her illuminated the dusty corners of the big upstairs room. Even with the wall sconces lighted and the heavy curtains drawn back to admit faint daylight through the tall streaked windows, there was little light.

The drawers in the chests and the shelves of the bookcases held the archduke's past, with surprising little footnotes to history scattered through the papers and books. She paused to read some of the yellowing letters carefully tied in bundles. They were in French, German, Italian, and some Slavic languages she could understand not at all. Many seemed to have been written to the archduke's forebears—his father, an uncle—and were signed with flourishes: a deposed king from the Balkans, a crown prince from a country that vanished during the Great War, an ambassador or two, generals and admirals and statesmen. There were letters about Niklas's military activities during the Second World War, suggesting daring and dangerous feats. Then there were passionate notes to the young Niklas on fine, pale paper that ought still to have smelled of lavender and rose petals but did not: a baroness in love, a woman who styled herself a princess, a once-famous film star. She kept the letters aside to take away as mementos of the old man. She also retained the decorations, although few of them turned out to be real gold or silver. Some of the musty old books went into a carton. There were various legal documents, but since—in spite of what she had told the seekers after the land—she was already in possession of the deed, she saved them for a later time.

Emma's things were of little interest. The clothes, the knicknacks, the old bills and tax returns Margaret stuffed into a large plastic bag to sort out at home.

Margaret went to the floor below, where the archduke had spent his time. The big portrait in the sitting room might have some value. She saw a remote resemblance to the archduke in the long-nosed, firm-chinned features of the subject. The frame itself was certainly grand.

As she was putting water on to boil for a sustaining cup of tea to help her through her chores, she heard Marcus's footsteps above.

She almost called out to him, but stopped herself. There was no point in starting a futile chase from room to room, floor to floor. She started back along the hallway past the archduke's bedroom and sitting room, and then stopped, a tremor of fear passing through her. Marcus had no keys.

But someone had gotten in last week, the late-night intruder that had been reported to the police. There might have been someone the day the archduke died, whether murderer or mere plunderer. She reminded herself that Marcus had surely learned many skills in the process of growing up in his world. A simple locked door or two would not stop him.

There was noise from above. Not footsteps, more like someone shifting boxes, opening drawers. Surely not Marcus, then. Someone looking for something in the cartons she had already begun to pack.

Who did I tell I was coming here? she thought. Did I mention it was to be today? Whoever is upstairs must know I am here.

She tried to move quietly along the hallway toward the stairs, then stopped. Someone had not hesitated to murder Emma, Lady Ross. Why not add Lady Margaret Priam to the list? She would not boldly go up the main stairs, she decided, but up the narrow back steps from the kitchen.

She tried to proceed very quietly now, still hoping that Marcus had found his way in and was perusing the historical documents relating to the Archduke Niklas's noble forebears. It seemed unlikely, but it gave her courage. Each creaking step on the back stairs made her heart pound harder.

"This is really irresponsible," she said under her breath, and flung open the door of the passageway into the big dim room.

A figure swathed in black garments was poised to plunge down the other stairs, toward the archduke's private lair.

Margaret was close to the front door and escape, so she was emboldened to shout sternly, "Stop!"

It had no effect on the intruder, who rapidly disappeared down the stairs.

Margaret tested her nerves. Yes, she was a bit frightened, but the adrenaline was flowing. It might or might not be Emma's murderer—indeed, there was nothing to indicate who it was wearing what looked like the archduke's cape, or widow's weeds, or a monkish robe.

She glanced about the cluttered room for a defensive weapon. Bless the archduke and his ancestors. Propped up in a corner behind an ornate, faded sofa was a tall ceremonial sword, complete with tarnished braid. The very sword, it seemed, on which the noble figure in the portrait below rested his hand. She pulled it from its sheath and the metal blade gleamed like new.

Sword in hand, she crossed the room and again descended the main staircase.

The person was in the archduke's sitting room now, making an unseemly amount of noise. There was very little light in the hall, and Margaret had left her flashlight somewhere along the way.

"Kindly show yourself," Margaret said from outside the door. She listened and heard: swish, rip, slash.

Should she try to retreat in dignity to the safety of upstairs and the door to the ordinary world?

But Priams do not retreat. Never: The Battle of Hastings, the Charge of the Light Brigade, the Somme and the Marne, the Battle of Britain. She pushed open the door with the point of her sword.

Out of the dimly lighted room flew the figure in black. Behind it the room was a tumble and the archduke's ancestral portrait shredded in its frame by the furious slashes of a knife. Margaret tried to step aside from the onrushing person, but the black-gloved hand that held the knife slashed in an arc.

Margaret saw the thin line of blood on the flesh of her arm. She saw it begin to well up and felt a stinging pain. She staggered back, knowing that something fairly bad had happened. The person in black fled, trailing robes.

Margaret leaned against the wall and looked at her arm. Was it deep and deadly or merely messy? She was trembling as she held the sword before her in her left hand now, and made her way upstairs. Had her assailant departed, or was the knife waiting to slash again?

Someone was pounding on the door. Bravely she grasped the knob and opened it.

"Aw man, you been in a knife fight?" Marcus was clearly taken aback at the sight of her bloodied arm. "You bad? You get him with that thing?"

Margaret shook her head and dropped the sword. "I'm so sorry. It seems that someone was here, but is gone now."

"You mean the one who just ran out? *She* cut you?"

"She? Who was it?" Margaret was beginning to feel light-headed from shock.

"Never mind," Marcus said. "You bleeding all over this floor." He was hustling her out of the building. "Where's your car? It's okay, I can drive."

"Who was it?" Margaret said again.

"I saw her at the boat that night." He made a gesture that conveyed the idea of a more than ample bosom. It could not be Tina, delectable as Paul found her, or the fleshless Belinda.

"Marie? But that's not right."

"I know what I saw. Move," he said. "I ain't going to have another one die on me."

They got to New York Hospital's emergency room. The barely post-pubescent intern who came to her aid looked askance at Margaret's unlikely companion, but she managed to reassure him. "Marcus is my . . . my bodyguard, who rescued me from . . . an accident. Could we do something about this cut?"

The youthful doctor said he was planning on becoming a plastic surgeon, and since business was slow in the ER just then, he could do a really good job with the stitches.

"Won't be any scar to speak of," he said, "maybe just a thin white line. This will be a great job. Trust me."

"Oh, I do," Margaret said, not trusting the child a bit.

Marcus was waiting for her at her car when she emerged from the emergency room, a hefty bandage protecting the stitches.

"Tell me again about the woman," she said as she sank into the car seat and closed her eyes. She was monumentally tired. "Tell me about Marie."

"Don't know no Marie," Marcus said. "I know who I saw. She had this black thing on, with another thing over her head, but when she shoved by me, the head thing . . ."

"Hood. It was a hood, I remember."

"Anyhow, she pushed it back, and I saw her clear, just the way I did when I was hanging around that car near the boat. She came with . . ." He scowled at the traffic.

"She came with Kenny Smith that night," Margaret said. "You don't know him."

Marcus was silent until they reached the underground garage in her building. When they parked in her space, she got out and stood up, very groggy now from the medications the doctor had stuffed into her.

"There's a door to the street over there," she said. "I'll be all right. I'll take the elevator up."

"Wait," Marcus said. "I forgot. About that mask thing. First the girl said it wasn't ready. Then this dude comes out and wants you to pick it up yourself to see if it's all right. But I know him. He's the one from the boat that night, right?"

"Right. Kenny. You did see him."

"I think I better see you get up to your place. You feelin' okay? I got to tell you something."

"Now?"

"Yeah, man, right now."

Later, when she was alone and drifting in and out of a feverish sleep and her arm throbbed, she tried to sort out what Marcus had told her. The last thing she remembered thinking before she fell into a deep sleep was that she rather missed the archduke, and what a pity it was he who was gone and the others were still about.

And they were all still about, in force. In the days following the incident at the archduke's apartment, about which only three people knew the actual facts, simply everyone knew something.

"I heard you tripped and fell while clearin' out the old archduke's place," Dalton said when he rang her.

"Did Marie tell you that?" Margaret said. "And thanks awfully for the flowers."

"Marie? I don't remember jes' where I heard," he said. "You going to be able to dance a two-step with me at this fancy party?"

"Sure will," Margaret said.

Belinda was mildly curious, but was rather more taken up with the crises and activities surrounding the masquerade. "Heard you were taken ill," she said. "Listen, Kenny thinks we ought to serve ortolans. Little bitsy birds, can you imagine it? It's late in the day to make changes, but the caterer says he can supply them. Do you think it's appropriate?"

"I believe they are very expensive," Margaret said.

"Kenny is spending money as though he had it," Belinda said.

"In any event, I don't believe ortolans are readily available in this country. I suggest you put a stop to the idea. The caterer would be charging for something that can't be provided."

"You're so sensible, Margaret. I do wish you were about to control Kenny."

"He once asked me to work for him," Margaret said, "but I thought better of it."

"You are going to be able to appear?" Belinda asked anxiously. "Good names are so important."

"Definitely," Margaret said.

Paul was one of the few people she admitted for a personal visit. When he was sprawled comfortably in one of the big soft chintz-covered chairs near the window that glimpsed the East River, he said, "Tina said you were severely injured, but that doesn't look like much."

"It's healing," Margaret said, "but I shall bear a mysterious scar. Did Tina mention that the injury was the result of an unprovoked attack by Marie d'Avalon? It was while I was clearing out the archduke's apartment, and she was skulking about unbeknownst to me. She must have been enraged by his new will."

"Or she expected that you were about to name her as Emma's murderer and wished to prevent you."

"I don't think that was it," Margaret said.

"Then why was she there?"

"Probably looking for the deed to that land, and whatever valuable knicknacks she could pocket."

"And did she find anything?"

"Nothing," Margaret said. "The archduke thoughtfully enclosed the deed with the copy of his will. I took the only thing of value early on, the emerald ring."

"But was it also Marie in the archduke's apartment the day he died? And if she has these violent tendencies, does this mean that she might have contrived the archduke's death as well?" Then he added firmly, "Margaret, you must inform the police."

"I continue to believe that the archduke died naturally," she said, "but Marie was my first thought in Emma's murder. However, I have stronger suspicions of another, confirmed by my colleague Marcus. No, I am not going to tell you, because I have no real proof at all. I'm certain Marie will ring me and explain herself. Everyone else has called. Both Norman Hope and Yale sent flowers. Kenny tried to see me, but I don't want visitors. There's a kind of minor conspiracy going on, but no one really knows who did the evil deed.''

"Have you told De Vere about your injury?"

"I told him a tale or two. He was concerned," Margaret said. "He believes I tripped over a rug and sprained an ankle."

"Margaret, you cannot have an open and loving relationship with a very fine man if you do not confess all of your misdeeds." Paul was very serious.

"How male of you to say so," Margaret said. "Do you confess all of your misdeeds to your loving ladies?"

Paul looked shocked. "Naturally not. That is different."

Margaret laughed. "What a dear boy you are. Are you prepared for *Feathers and Fashion*? It's only two days off."

"I am prepared," Paul said. "The Ferrari is throbbing with eagerness, polished and scented. I wish you would announce who precisely is the murderer, since I would like to deepen my relationship with Tina, but I hesitate until I know if she is likely to take a weapon to me."

"Please don't continue to pin your romantic hopes on Tina," Margaret said. "And I will try to have all this straightened out in a few days, right after the ball." She reached out to answer her ringing phone.

"Yes. No. Yes," was all Paul heard her say.

When she had hung up, Margaret sighed and said, "Marie claims to have just returned from an extended tour of the countryside, collecting roots and berries for her beauty preparations. She has just heard that I was injured by a city bus, and sends her best wishes for a quick recovery. What a wonder she is."

Chapter 22

Margaret *tried* on the mask that Marcus had finally managed to extract from Kenny Smith. It glittered with points of amethyst and plum-colored rhinestones and sequins, and it was edged with purple and black feathers that sprayed out on either side of her head. It was very glamorous. It complemented perfectly the strapless deep purple evening gown of satin that Margaret had paid a good deal of money for because she loved it on sight, but that there were too few occasions to wear. Kenny's fête was just right. To cover the thin bandage that protected her healing knife cut, Margaret planned to wear long kid gloves that reached her elbow.

It was the day, and nearly the hour now, for her to venture out to the ball. Margaret was forced to push back sudden rushes of nerves because tonight she would make a statement that could not be ignored, and then she would have to tell someone like De Vere what her suspicions were, frail though the evidence was.

She had seen De Vere the day before to confess the true nature of her injury. He had not been pleased. She had not told him that Marie had taken a dagger to her, since she had come to believe that Marie had merely been annoyed, not murderous.

"What if it came to me that I knew who had killed Emma Ross but had no proof?" Margaret had asked him.

"A lot of murders are officially unsolved," he said. "What do you know?"

"Nothing. Sometimes the pieces fit together, and you know."

"Tell me when the pieces fit," he said. "And I am grateful that you don't expect me to take you to this ball."

Now she swished her train, straightened her mask, and opened the door to Yale Dalton.

Alas, the white limo sometimes dedicated to the glory of the Hopes and therefore to Yale Dalton did not speed them to the door of the old and distinguished men's club that was the site of Kenny's party. Margaret wondered if relations between the Hopes and Dalton were strained—or perhaps it was relations between Norman and his friend from the old neighborhood who was tired of loaning out a limo that could be carrying high-paying customers.

Yale and Margaret arrived at the ponderous portals of the club where Kenny's party was being held in a more modest towncar.

In the spacious entrance hall, a short, broad flight of stairs led up from the dark-paneled reception area, to wide open doors of a room that had been turned into a ballroom for the occasion. Margaret saw a cluster of befeathered guests about to enter, and she could hear the sounds of a fairly decorous musical group.

The heavy doors off the entrance hall were closed to keep out curious nonmembers who might want to pry into life behind the secrets of the club. She supposed this went back to the days when woman-shy gentlemen had constructed the place as a safe haven for themselves. As an additional deterrent to nonmember frivolity, solemn time-darkened portraits of bearded men frowned down on the gaily costumed arrivals.

"This sure looks like it's goin' to be fine," Yale Dalton said. His concession to costume was a broad-brimmed western hat with an eagle feature tucked in the headband. He had shown Margaret a black half mask, and then had shaken his head and put it away in a pocket.

"Very nice," Margaret murmured. "Kenny will be gratified by the numbers."

"What sorta place is this?" Dalton asked. He squinted up at a portrait of a nineteenth-century merchant banker who looked shocked to see so many ladies invading these sacred halls.

"Gentleman's club originally," Margaret said. "I understand that they are required now to admit women, although they are said to invite only very old and distinguished ladies who do not get about much anymore, and will therefore not disturb tradition too severely. A good deal of important business is discussed here, you know, and it is not a good idea to let the women understand too much of what is going on, lest they come out ahead."

"Speakin' of business," Yale said, "you had much of a chance to think over what's going to be done with the archduke's property?" He tried to sound offhanded, but Margaret knew he really wanted to know.

"I have just about decided," Margaret said. "We ought to meet and talk it over—but not tonight. Tomorrow or the next day?"

"Whatever you say," Yale said. He offered his arm, and they ascended the stairs to find the ballroom before them. It was already quite crowded with costumed revelers who felt no shame in dressing up in outlandish garments, many of them utilizing feathers.

Kendall Smith could be seen at the end of the room on a raised platform that held a table piled high with many copies of *Feathers and Fashion Through History*. Like many of the male guests, Kenny had not succumbed to the lure of dressing up. He wore evening dress, and a shocking pink turban topped by a spray of peacock feathers and a large aquamarine brooch. The ladies, however, had found the appeal of a masquerade more than their good sense could manage. Marie Antoinette, or someone very like her, was seen in several parts of the room. Perhaps the scales had been tipped in the direction of the late eighteenth century by the opportunity to wear towering white wigs and shamelessly low-cut gowns re-

vealing newly augmented breasts encased in tight satin bod-
ices.

"Well, ain't this something?" Yale said. "That old Wayne
over there? And is that big ol' bird with him Marie?"

The "big ol' bird" was indeed Marie, decked out in Kenny
Smith's Firebird costume. It was an elaborate creation with
a flowing chiffon skirt in brilliant red and a full mask that
boasted a long gilded beak and sprays of crimson and gold
feathers atop her head. She looked rather ferocious.

"Spectacular," Margaret murmured. She hoped she
would not have to engage in idle party chat with her attacker.
Long shining red talons on each of Marie's fingers reminded
Margaret that if Marie was moved to slash the ancestral portrait of a man who had done her wrong, how easy the tran-
sition to slashing Margaret who had done nothing at all.

"Well, what happens next?" Yale asked. "We got to talk
to anybody or shake hands, or just go off and dance?"

"I suppose we ought to go round and say a word to Kenny,
and Belinda Hope who planned all this. But first I'd like to
run across to have a word with a friend I see. Dianne Stark.
You must know of her husband, Charles Stark, the finan-
cier."

"That's a name I've heard," Yale said. "You run along.
I'll catch up with you after I speak to the lady and Kenny."

Dianne was across the room. She had decided to commit
herself to a sort of costume after all, and was wearing a 1930s
movie-star gown that Jean Harlow would have envied, with
lots of feather trim and a trailing boa. But it wasn't Dianne
that Margaret went to first. Rather she headed toward a dark-
skinned masked pasha with a white plume in his turban and
shiny white pantaloons and an embroidered vest showing an
admirable expanse of chest. Marcus had arrived, to guard
Margaret.

"I *am* relieved to see you," Margaret said. "I never expected to need a bodyguard when we were first doing business, but things do change rather quickly."

Marcus shifted his shoulders. "At least nobody I know's
going to see me," he said. He straightened his turban.

"It won't be difficult to keep track of Marie," Margaret

said. "She's in red, and she has the biggest headdress in the place."

"She ain't the one you got to worry about," Marcus said. "Here come some friends of yours." He edged behind one of the club's rubber plants and disappeared from view.

"Margaret darling! Isn't this fantastic?" Belinda Hope had wisely rejected Marie Antoinette and had chosen instead to appear as a flapper in a glittery long-waisted dress with a tall aigrette rising from a jeweled band circling her head. "You look divine!" Her enthusiasm had a touch of envy. "And look at Dianne!"

"You do like nice," Margaret said to Dianne. "Is that a vintage dress or did you just dream it up? And how is Charlie coping with all this?"

"Authentic 1935," Dianne said. "Don't you love it? And Charlie amazes me. He agreed to dress up like a what-do-you-call-it? A cavalier, with a big feather in his hat and a Vandyke beard. Unheard of behavior, but it must be a relief to do something silly, after being so serious about money all the time."

"Rather like the way Malcolm Forbes used to go ballooning over France or ride his motorcycle about Manhattan," Margaret said.

Belinda hated to be left out. "Kenny is simply thrilled at the response," she said. "People are actually buying his book, and we sold enough tickets to cover quite a few of the expenses. He insisted on far too many free tickets being handed out, so there won't be much for the charity, but they were a bit nervous about the feathers business in the end, so it all works out perfectly."

Belinda stopped to take a breath, and Margaret said quickly, "Isn't that Norman Mailer just coming in?" It wasn't, of course, but it was enough to send Belinda flying to greet new arrivals.

"It looks more like Paul Castrocani," Dianne said.

"Yes," Margaret said, "and Tina Corrado, dressed as an angel. Now that's ironic."

Tina wore cunning little feathery wings and a gauzy but

somehow sexy gown. Paul had taken Margaret's advice and had worn tails, a princely penguin.

"How can Kenny afford all this?" Dianne said. "You know he paid to have that book published, and he's paying for most of tonight. I heard that from very good sources. And is it true that he had some kind of disastrous showing of his new line the other day? I didn't read anything about it, but someone I know was there. Very bad if he hopes to market his things on a wide scale. People do talk so."

"It was not inspiring," Margaret said. "I'm afraid that his expectations of financial backing are fading rapidly. And worse may be yet to come." Kenny was still smiling and nodding, collecting cash and checks and signing his name to his books with a flourish.

"If you ask me," Dianne said, "it takes a huge ego to think you can compete from the ground up with the big boys and girls in the fashion game."

"His ego is very large indeed," Margaret said.

"What is this rumor that you've suddenly become very wealthy via an inheritance? I said it couldn't be so, or you would have called Charlie at once for advice."

"Not true, alas," Margaret said. "I was touched that Archduke Niklas decided to make the gesture. He wrote a lovely little letter saying that he wanted what he had to go to a person of his social class. Snobbish to the end, but I do understand the sentiments of the old school. He didn't expect to pass it on to me so soon."

Margaret was distracted by the sight of the Dalton gang clustered around Kenny on the dais. Yale, Tina, and Wayne surrounded him. Marie had taken off her probably suffocating Firebird mask, and was trying to wedge her way into the conversation, along with Belinda and Norman (a dispirited looking Cock Robin for the occasion). Photographers had converged on the book-signing table, and the frequent flashes indicated that there would be enough photos to find their way into a few glossy publications, or at least Kenny Smith's publicity portfolio. Margaret was kind enough to allow Kenny his brilliant moment, but soon enough she would have put them all on notice that she would have to state her suspicions.

She took a deep breath and approached the dais. Paul was standing nearby awaiting the release of Tina to him. Behind him, a tall black youth nodded his turban, folded his arms across his chest, and watched.

"Kenny, everyone," she said loudly enough to catch their attention. "Since you're all together, I want to tell you that I know about Emma. I believe I can prove it, and I intend to share my information. I won't disrupt this evening, but tomorrow . . ."

There was a brilliant flash behind her, and an unknown photographer caught the entire group open-mouthed and wide-eyed in stunned surprise at her announcement.

"Shall we have a dance, Paul?" she said. "It's a pity to waste this lovely music."

Paul had been rendered speechless, and offered his arm to lead her onto the dance floor. He found his voice as they swept into a waltz that set the panniered gowns of the numerous eighteenth-century lovelies swaying.

"You have threatened them," Paul said. "But you do not immediately bring the killer to justice."

"Paul dear, have you forgotten how difficult justice is? Especially with the kind of flimsy proof I hold. I am hoping that the guilty party will take the opportunity to vanish, or confess. . . ."

"Or do you harm. Did you consider that possibility?"

"I have protection," Margaret said. Marcus hovered at the edge of the dance floor, taking seriously his duties as a bodyguard. "And my protection knows who it is he must watch. I will be all right."

In this matter, however, Margaret was rather too optimistic.

Chapter 23

The idea of an immense masquerade party appeared to have captured the fancy of a large number of people who otherwise would have shown better sense. More and more costumed fun-seekers packed the floor, feathers flying. Margaret would not have been surprised to learn that several statuesque women were actually statuesque men, but that was what made Manhattan the wonderful place it was. Maharajahs jostled show girls bedecked in feathers, Madame de Pompadour gossiped with a Hawaiian king in a feathered robe. There were native American war bonnets aplenty and even an extravagant reproduction of the Aubrey Beardsley peacock cape.

Paul released Margaret to Yale Dalton with a look of caution, but Margaret merely smiled and danced away with him.

"You mean what you said just now?" Yale asked. "You know who murdered poor Emma?"

"Oh yes," Margaret said. "Don't you?"

"Why, if I did, I would tell the police," he said. He was not convincing.

"I think not," Margaret said, "unless your background can stand up to a really close investigation."

"There is that," Yale said. "It's not been easy bein' questioned. I wonder where Marie has got to? There's ol' Wayne standing off all alone." Dalton was clearly eager to free himself of Margaret for a time to confer with his associate. Kenny intruded and gave Yale the opportunity to depart, rather hastily, in Wayne's direction.

"I was stunned by your announcement," Kenny said, peering at her closely through his round glasses. "You actually *know*? Proof and everything?"

"The proof is rather insubstantial, but it points in a definite direction." Margaret sighed. "It's a pity Emma didn't live to see your party. She loved to pretend she was someone else."

"She did love to pretend," Kenny said. "That is true."

"And you'll get lovely publicity for the fête. I'm sure Poppy will mention it, and it's sure to be written up other places."

"Expensive, though," Kenny said. "Very expensive. I must rush off and sign more books. It's going to be a collector's item."

Now Margaret was alone in the midst of the revelry. Most faces were masked, and those she knew had vanished. Marcus was surely somewhere on guard, although she could not spot him with so many dancers taking advantage of a sudden noisy turn to a disco beat. She ducked under waving arms and avoided flailing feet to find a haven at the side of the dance floor. The two long sides of the ballroom were semi-hallways with a row of widely spaced columns to divide the passageway from the big room. Darkened corridors leading into the depths of the building opened off the opposite side of the hall space. Decorous dark maroon velvet ropes across the doorways were designed to remind the ballgoers that those parts of the club were off limits.

Margaret wandered down the length of the passageway toward the back of the ballroom. Now and then a dancer or two slipped off the dance floor and passed her on the way to the lounges down the main staircase. She understood that on the opposite side of the ballroom two large rooms were reserved for a midnight buffet (presumably without ortolans) and the bar.

"Ssss."

Margaret looked up from her thoughts at the sound. Someone appeared to be trying to attract another's attention.

"Ssss . . ." The sound again. Margaret looked around. There was no one in the passageway, and all the dancers out beyond the columns looked dazed as they rocked, rolled, and gyrated. Suddenly a dimmish light was turned on at the end of the corridor off the passage where Margaret was standing.

She peered down the corridor and saw a flash of red feathers. Then the Firebird stepped into the light at the end of the corridor and beckoned. The golden glitter on the fiercely beaked mask glinted, and the crimson sprays of feathers atop the mask shimmered.

Margaret shook her head. She was not foolish enough to go off into the dark reaches of the club with Marie d'Avalon. Marie, apparently, did not accept her refusal. The Firebird approached. Margaret looked about for Marcus, but saw no sign of him. She decided to seek her safety in numbers. With the wild scene on the dance floor, no one would be bothered about a dancer without a partner. She edged into the crowd and danced her way across to the other side. Somehow Kenny managed to have had flashing colored strobe lights installed to take over from the stately crystal chandeliers, so the shapes and faces of the dancers in their bizarre masks were suddenly illuminated and then as quickly lost in darkness.

"Oops, so sorry." Margaret knocked a wig askew, trod on a satiny toe, tripped on a trailing gown. Then the lights above flashed on, and she saw the bright red Firebird advancing toward her through the dancers.

Surely Marie was not still so bent on revenge for having lost out on the archduke's land to do something truly foolish in the midst of all these people. She had been so certain that Marie had not murdered Emma, yet she could almost feel the single-minded intensity of her pursuer.

She reversed direction and ducked between a woman all in streaming black feathers and a half-naked native American warrior. Over her shoulder, she saw that the Firebird still trailed her. She was worried now. Marcus, wherever he was, had not been told to watch Marie, but someone else.

She thought if she could disentangle herself from the dance floor, where she realized she could be trapped by the sheer mass of the revelers, she could make her way down to the foyer level. There would be space and many people coming and going, and she could confront Marie in comparative safety.

Then she came face to face with Marie.

Not the Firebird who was pursuing her, but Marie d'Avalon herself, still decked out in her red feathers and flowing chiffon, but without the mask.

"I want to speak to you," Marie said, "about these rrrrumors. I do not stab even my enemies in the back. . . ."

"Later," Margaret said. The Firebird was very close now.

"Aha!" Marie said. "Another Firebird? How dare Kendall duplicate . . ." But Margaret fled onward toward the broad stairs.

She flung aside her mask as she rushed down the stairs, but her hope for safety in the company of resting party-goers was in vain. The huge hall was empty and the Firebird was closer, and instead of the long bloodred talons that Marie wore, the Firebird held a long dagger. It was not to be strangulation then, as in the case of Emma, but a quick stab and a pool of blood.

The Firebird stopped and descended the last steps slowly.

Margaret stared into the slanted eyes of the fierce mask and saw the light from the hanging chandelier reflected back.

She didn't hesitate, but held up her purple skirt and ran behind the broad staircase, down a dark hallway. In the darkness, she felt for a door and found a doorknob, turned it, and slammed the door behind her. Her hand touched a big old-fashioned key in the lock. She turned it, tested the door, and breathed a sigh of relief. She was safe for the moment, locked into what appeared to be a library or reading room.

She stumbled over an armchair and found a table lamp. The small circle of light was comforting. The walls were lined with leather-bound volumes, and a long polished table held magazines and newspapers. An ornate marble fireplace took up most of one side of the room, and there was an aroma of a century of fine cigars and pipe smoke bonded to the very air of the room.

Of course there was no telephone. A club servant undoubtedly answered calls elsewhere and conveyed messages to the elderly gentlemen who dozed in the leather armchairs behind their newspapers. Well, she was safe for the moment.

Then she was not safe. A low door beside the fireplace opened, and the Firebird entered.

Kenny Smith pushed back the mask and shook his head. "This is absolutely *perfect*! I couldn't have thought of a better place myself. How lucky to find the servant's door." He started toward her. "You know I can't allow you to ruin my plans," he said, "just as I couldn't allow Emma to do so. And now no one is going to be able to figure out what happened to you, alone and dead in this room."

"Marie saw you," Margaret said.

"Marie saw another Firebird. Someone in red who found the mask she had abandoned. Honestly, Margaret, I didn't plan it this way, it just worked out." He held out the dagger. "I mean, I had brought along a few bits and pieces in case Marie's costume needed repairs. Instead of a dress, I had this big piece of the fabric I'd used for Marie." He slipped off the enfolding red chiffon robe. "You said you knew the murderer, and you were going to tell, so I just improvised. I am one of the great improvisers." He was edging nearer to her. "I improvised with the pillow and the archduke, too."

"They'll know," Margaret said. "And Marcus knows. He saw you coming out of Emma's place right after the murder, and then saw you going in again later. I have your coat. He saw that too, on the chair."

"The police will never to able to prove it."

"It's a start," Margaret said, getting a little desperate. "And besides, Marcus is here and has been watching you all evening."

"Me, perhaps, but not the Firebird."

"There's more," she said very slowly, hoping to buy a few more seconds. "The costume you made for Emma. You brought it along for her to try on the night you murdered her. She must have taken off Marie's dress, because one doesn't think twice about disrobing in the presence of one's dress designer. Perhaps as she was trying on the costume, she told you that Dalton was out to cheat everyone, and she wouldn't allow the archduke to sell his land to him. All her high-flown promises to you about backers and money and land had come to nothing. And when she was dead, you removed the costume and put the robe on her.''

Kenny was close to Margaret now, and the dagger looked very dangerous. ''Almost right,'' he said. ''Although I was simply *aghast* at what she'd done to the hem. I told her I'd fix it up while she tried on the costume.''

Margaret backed away a step. It was beginning to look very serious. ''You must already have known that things were going wrong with Dalton. You came to Emma's prepared to kill her.''

''Please, dear, of course I did. Emma had been hinting and hinting about being in a position to ruin my plans. I have never hesitated to put a dead stop to anyone who interferes with my business.'' Kenny moved fast. He raised his arm to plunge the dagger into Margaret's expensively clothed chest.

But Marcus was moving faster, slipping through the small door behind Kenny's back. He lunged and grabbed Kenny from behind, while Margaret tried to shield herself with her already damaged arm. She felt a sharp pain as Kenny's dagger missed her heart but sliced into almost the same spot where Marie had cut her.

''See here!'' a loud voice said. ''Absolutely *no* women are allowed in this room!''

As she fell, she saw the indignant club guardian at the open door, scowling furiously as the serious transgression of a female in the sacred male haven.

Chapter 24

"*I*t's all right now," De Vere said. "Very little damage done to you." He was so relieved that he resisted berating her for her folly, or even mentioning that she had definitely promised him never again to become involved in murder.

Marcus and Paul had seen that she was stitched up again, and had brought her home. Paul had summoned De Vere, who found her drowsing in bed resting her bandaged arm on a pillow.

"It was terribly foolish of me," Margaret said. She reached out with her good arm and took his hand. "I'm awfully glad you're here, Sam."

"I'm glad that *you* are here. You could have been very dead, and you're too important for me to lose."

"But there was no proof at all, unless Kenny tried to kill me, if not at the ball then elsewhere. Until I spoke up, maybe he expected to get away with two murders. As you say, many murders go unsolved. With his ego, he felt that removing obstacles by murder was a mere unpleasant necessity, and if Dalton failed him, he'd find other backers." She sighed. "At least we are spared Kenny: The Fragrance."

"My colleagues will take another very close look at everything. You shouldn't have kept his coat and that costume, you know. We could have run tests."

"Tests! Ha! The only real proof was Marcus seeing Kenny

199

come out of Emma's building early and then returning as a guest later. Are you telling me that you would have paid much attention to the ravings of your prime suspect?''

''We might have listened to Marcus in the end,'' De Vere said. ''But except for the damage done to you, this is rather better.'' He stood up and looked down at her. ''Margaret,'' he said seriously, ''a man does not like to think that the next time he sees the woman he loves, she will be a murder victim. I know this is New York, and things do happen, but . . .''

''But they'd better not happen to me? Agreed. However, since I am not at my best tonight, ought we mention love?'' She closed her eyes so as not to deal with his rare statement about his feeling toward her. ''Here's a promise: I will behave.'' She opened her eyes. ''There is one bad thing about this mess. Poor Norman won't be rich enough for Belinda to divorce, and they'll go on and on and on. . . .'' Margaret yawned. The tranquilizer the doctor had given her was putting her to sleep. ''Oh, dear. Another bad thing. I fear dear Paul will find that his lovely Tina has quickly packed up and fled with Dalton and Wayne. I wouldn't be surprised to find that all along she was Mrs. Yale Dalton or whatever his name is. But there is also one good thing. Two good things. No, three.''

''They are?''

''Marcus is a hero, and he has a job with Kasparian as long as he wants it. That's one. Two is that before the nastiness in the library, Dianne Stark bought me a copy of Kenny's book. Autographed. It's sure to be a collector's item.''

''Three?''

''Three is the archduke's land. I really must make amends for *Feathers and Fashion*. I plan to look into donating that piece of desert to a conservationist group so the baby quail can frolic under the cacti forever undisturbed.''

About the Author

JOYCE CHRISTMAS has written five previous novels: *Hidden Assets* (with Jon Peterson), *Blood Child*, *Dark Tide*, *Suddenly In Her Sorbet*, and *Simply to Die For*. In addition, she has spent a number of years as a book and magazine editor. She lives in a part of New York City where as yet Society rarely sets foot.

White-haired grandmother...

&

free-lance CIA agent...

DOROTHY GILMAN'S
Mrs. Pollifax Novels